FI

The man took
'I'll kill you.'

McAllister s
the man twice, mouth and
once on the nose. The last made a
surprising amount of noise.

The man's voice sounded a little mushy when he said: 'That won't do you no good. I'm still going to kill you.'

He aimed a kick for McAllister's crotch. McAllister batted the foot aside and hit the man on the neck. The blow staggered him backwards.

McAllister said: 'You're not two-twenty pounds of muscle and bone. You're just full of crap.'

The man charged and McAllister thought: *If he gets those arms around me, I'm finished.*

The man got his arms around him and he heard his ribs crack. The man tightened his grip and said: 'I told you I was going to kill you, you bastard.'

Further McALLISTER Westerns
in Hamlyn Paperbacks

McALLISTER ON THE COMANCHE CROSSING
McALLISTER AND THE SPANISH GOLD
McALLISTER NEVER SURRENDERS
McALLISTER AND CHEYENNE DEATH
QUARRY
DIE-HARD
WOLF-BAIT

McAllister
in
FIRE-BRAND

Matt Chisholm

Hamlyn Paperbacks

FIRE-BRAND
ISBN 0 600 20519 3

First published in Great Britain 1983
by Hamlyn Paperbacks

Hamlyn Paperbacks are published by
The Hamlyn Publishing Group Ltd.,
Astronaut House,
Feltham, Middlesex, England.

Made and printed in Great Britain by
Cox & Wyman Ltd, Reading

1

The town of Black Horse, you might say, was the heart of the Black Horse country. If you said that, you would have to admit that Tully's back room was the heart of Black Horse town.

Tully's, of course, was a saloon and a not too salubrious one at that. Through the years it had many a name painted over its shabby porticos – The Last Chance, the Golden Nugget, Lucky Lady, and so on and so forth. No matter what was up there, everybody still went on calling it just plain Tully's.

That was because Mark Tully was a character.

Some of the old-timers could still remember the rakehelly days of Mark's youth when, though he had never been what you might call downright evil, he was pretty wild. But it was not his wildness which made him so formidable, it was his skill with guns. Men said, no matter where he carried a gun, he could always produce it twice as fast as any other man alive. And once he had produced it, he showed his skill of hitting a target without appearing to take any kind of aim.

Now Mark was in his middle years and had put behind him any thought of wild adventure, contenting himself with occasionally allowing himself to be sworn in as a member of a sheriff's posse.

The sheriff in question was Remington McAllister, another stalwart of the circle which met in Tully's back room of a Saturday night. Well, that was where they met in the winter, because there the stove glowed warm and held off the bitter cold of these northern climes. Come summer, the cronies would sit on the sidewalk outside the saloon, pipes, cigarettes and cigars loading the night air with their pungent aromas. Some ultra-respectable citizens (or their wives) had complained of this public display of the consumption of hard liquor, but certainly nothing was done about it while McAllister reigned in the sheriff's office.

These friends honoured me from time to time with inclusion within their circle, and I have to admit that I received more entertainment there in an hour than I had of a theatre in a whole evening. The stories were tall, the lies enormous and the talk often ploughed a deep furrow. There was a bit of everything at Tully's. I suppose the highlight of any evening was when Tully and McAllister began: 'Say, Mark, do you remember when . . . ?' Or 'McAllister, did you know that little rooster down in Live Oak County . . . ?' And then the flow of talk would come. Oldsters would sit back to listen and laugh; the youngsters held their tongues to learn. Tully and McAllister, men said, had seen it all.

Some of the stories were told more than once. Maybe there would be a newcomer in the group who had not had the opportunity of hearing some classic of the sageland sagas. In which case, the storyteller would say: 'If you fellows can stand it just one more time around . . .' and then he would be off.

One night, Lon McKenna the mayor, who ran the livery stable on Main, said: 'Young Jasper here didn't ever hear the story of how you eeloped with Mark's gal, Rem. Do you think you could oblige?'

This involved a story concerning Mark Tully and Remington McAllister in equal parts, so they usually told it, taking turn and turn-about, and they used to vie with each other on the amount of laughter they could evoke. It usually lasted about an hour and ended with men begging them to stop or they would suffer a busted gut. You could call it a bawdy story, though obscene might be a better word, and it entailed McAllister carrying off the girl's mother in error. There followed, indeed, a whole comedy of errors, in which the stolen woman fell madly in love with McAllister, who nearly got himself shot by the irate husband for stealing his wife. The whole was related by two men who were past-masters in the art of maintaining a poker-face.

By the time they were through and everyone lay about in their chairs wiping their eyes and holding their aching sides, men were declaring that it was the best they had ever heard it told. It was the spring of the year and this was the first night in which the circle had met in the open. Doc Robertson, as usual, was the first to make his apologies and retire. He had an early call, he said.

Colonel Ralph English, who owned the Grand Union Hotel, which he had won a few years before on the turn of a card, declared that it was time he got his beauty sleep. Lennie Wallach, who owned and ran the local newspaper, said he must go and put his paper to bed. McAllister said: 'Hold up, I'm coming your way, boys.' Thus Doc Robertson, Lennie Wallach and McAllister strolled down the middle of Main together in the bright moonlight, followed by the shouted farewells of their comfortably lubricated friends.

George Robertson said: 'As good an evening as ever I remember.'

Wallach said: 'I have not laughed so much before in all my life.'

McAllister said: 'That boy, Jasper – the one we told the story for – did either of you see him before?'

No, they said, not ever. Why did McAllister ask?

'Did you catch his last name?'

No, they said, they did not. Now he had their curiosity aroused. Again they wanted to know why he asked. McAllister's answer to that was simple – he did not know. They strolled on. They parted at the intersection between Main and Morrow.

Doc Robertson said: 'Bertha told me to offer you a bed for the night, Rem.'

'No, thanks all the same, George. I'll get back.'

Wallach said: 'Well, I'll say goodnight, boys. So long.'

They said 'So long, Lennie,' and the Jewish newspaperman walked away to his office. They could see the light burning in his window and the figure of his daughter, Debbie, bent over some task. The town was quiet. Scarcely anybody was out on the streets.

McAllister said: 'Bring Bertha out to see the horses, George. Have a meal.'

'Tuesday evening?'

'Fine.'

They lifted their hands to each other, as old friends will, and McAllister turned towards McKenna's livery. It occupied half a block on Main, consisting of a large stable and two extensive corrals. The mayor traded in horses, hired horses out and was now extending himself into general freighting. McKenna would be a big man one day.

As McAllister walked down the silent street and approached the main gate of the livery, he heard footsteps on the sidewalk behind him. Turning, he recognised the dim figure of the mayor himself. When he saw McAllister waiting, McKenna quickened his pace. He was a garrulous, friendly little man. To have been made mayor of Black Horse was the highest peak of his life.

'That was one great evening, Rem,' he said, chuckling. 'I guess I could hear that yarn a hundred times and not tire of it.'

'Who was that boy, Jasper, we told it for?' McAllister asked.

'Don't rightly know. Somebody's nephew, wasn't he?'

Then they were walking through the gateway and were in the yard of the livery. Tommy Shultz, McKenna's boy, was asleep in the hay. The mayor went to rouse him to get McAllister's horse, but the big man stopped him.

'I can still saddle a horse, Lon.'

McKenna gave him a hand saddling his canelo gelding, Oscar, and a moment later McAllister was aboard and telling the mayor goodnight. He took the horse at a steady walk through town, so as not to waken early sleepers, and did not lift it into a faster pace until he had crossed the creek by the lumber bridge and was out on to the plain beyond.

He followed the valley road as it swung towards the creek and, before it reached the creek, he turned away from it and started across his own land. There was a light breeze blowing along the valley and it was pleasantly refreshing on his face.

He rode with the quiet satisfaction of a man who has passed a few hours in the company of friends, tired after a long day and ready for his bed. As he came near the corrals, he heard a couple of his horses whinny a welcome. Oscar rumbled a reply. Drawing rein at the corral gate as the stud horse, Caesar, came and poked his great head over the gate rail at him.

It was then that McAllister heard the horse running in the night, going along the valley road. He wondered who that might be – somebody late from drinking in town? Mentally, he ticked off the names of men who lived down the valley and those he had known to be in town. There had been two. Keogh, who had left in the middle of the evening, and Duval, who had left shortly before himself. He heard the horse break pace as it turned down the road to the creek and then listened to the hoofbeats going north down the valley. Reckless riding for a man travelling at night, even if he knew the road.

He threw Oscar into the corral and, hearing the music of Mose Copley in the smithy, he turned his feet in that direction. Mose was making a fancy gate for Lisle Manning across the valley. Lisle had made a pile of money in cattle and he was spending accordingly, making his ranch-house into a mansion. Local folks were rather proud of it, the first great house in their country. They were proud of Lisle too, because he was a good cattleman and spent freely in town.

Mose grinned briefly as McAllister entered. He was medium-sized, but he packed a lot of strength and stamina in his hard body. His sweating flesh glistened black in the firelight. He worked for five minutes, completing what he had on hand, then laid aside his tools to discuss the day with his boss. His boy Lige was McAllister's solitary hired hand, a gangling boy in his 'teens, born to handle and understand horses. The Copleys had their cabin on the far side of the creek. Mose's wife Bella kept McAllister's house clean and cooked his meals. All in all, it was a good arrangement.

Mose said: 'You hear that man putting his horse along the valley top speed?'

'Sure.'

'Wonder who that can be.'

'Either he has urgent business or he's a damn fool to ride that way at night.'

And that was all they said about it that night. They discussed the limp one of the younger mares was showing, agreed that Caesar should take a rest after a number of mares had been put to him and agreed that the grass on the east side of the creek had never been better for hay. They would cut a bumper crop that year. McAllister told Mose goodnight and went to his bunk. He woke once in the night to hear a rider on the valley road again. This time he was going back towards town. McAllister wondered if it was the same man. Ordinarily, McAllister was a man who strictly minded his own business. But when you are county sheriff, you are paid to mind everybody else's. However, he dismissed the matter from his mind and turned over to go to sleep again. If he had not, there might not be any story to tell.

2

Wanlace & Co it said above the stage station. Under the control of Horry Wanlace, they ran a there-and-back coach run between the Black Horse country and the town of Caspar, Wyoming. It did the trip twice a week, carrying passengers, light goods and United States mail. It was a small outfit, but efficient, and it was starting to make money. Wanlace had ambitions and once a week tried to buy the mayor's freighting business from him. Together, they would be a good economic proposition. Maybe, Lon McKenna suggested, they should become partners; but Horry would have none of that. He liked to work alone.

It was Horry's boast that his little line had never been late, never lost a passenger and never been stopped successfully by a road agent. Some damn fool had tried to do it the year before, but he had been a bungler. Just as he was shouting: 'Throw down the strong-box,' he had tripped and shot himself in the foot. Horry had brought him in for medical treatment at the hands of Doc Robertson. An amused magistrate had fined him fifty dollars. When the man confessed that his worldly wealth consisted of his horse and saddle and that he did not have two cents to rub together (else why should he be crazy enough to rob a stage?) the same magistrate ordered horse and saddle sold to pay the fine. The erstwhile road agent now served the community as a swamper in Mark Tully's saloon.

This morning, as the stage waited for passengers and load outside the stage line office on Morrow, there came Ham Stoppard, the teller at the bank, to tell Horry Wanlace to hold his horses because there was a strong-box being sent by the bank to Caspar and beyond. The passengers climbed aboard and Horry, who was driving the team himself that day, started to make impatient sounds. However, as starting time was reached, Ham Stoppard and another sweating man bore a strong-box between them and heaved it aboard under the stern supervision of the banker himself, J. Howard Lindholm. 'Now, Horry,' he told the stage owner, 'you take good care of that. I hold you personally responsible, hear?'

Horry was cheerful enough about it. 'Dismiss your fears, J. Howard,' he said, 'this line has an impeccable record of safe-delivery. It shall reach Caspar safe and sound, my solemn word on it.'

'Just to be sure,' J. Howard declared, 'the bank's man, Hammond Stoppard, shall ride inside, armed and ready. Is that not so, Hammond?'

Hammond swallowed a couple of times – he was renowned for hating the sight and sound of guns – and agreed that he was as ready as he would ever be. He climbed inside the coach. Horry and his messenger, Wally Hunt, secured the strong-box in the boot, tied down the tarpaulin over it and climbed aboard. Horry did his imitation of the classic stage driver, cracking his whip and shouting. His six half-broken mustangs, having kicked and bitten each other without fear or favour a few times, finally agreed to hit their collars and raggedly pulled the stage out of town. By the time it reached the bridge over the creek, it was going a fair old pace and Horry was quite proud of it. It slowed a little for the steep grade up from the creek, but once it was on the valley road, it rocked along at a pace which was enough to turn any passenger's hair grey; and that in Horry's opinion, was the way in which every good stage driver drove.

'We are fifty seconds behind schedule,' he told Wally Hunt. 'Lateness ain't a thing I admire.'

'You would think,' Hunt said primly, 'that a banking man would know better.'

'Yes, indeedy,' said Horry.

They turned off the creek road on to the hill road to cross the valley on two wheels. Horry gave a piercing yell as they went round. One of the passengers turned to his companions and said dispassionately: 'Crazy bastard, what does he think he is, huh?' He was a well-to-do cattleman from the south end of the valley, stout-bellied now and doing most of his work from a buggy instead of a horse's back. Beside him sat a drummer in ladies' wear, heading back for Caspar and the bright lights beyond. He had travelled so extensively in stages that there was not a driver on the continent who could raise the smallest twinge of fear in him. He said: 'One thing I'll say for old Horry, he always gets you there on time.'

'Alive?' said the rancher.

The third occupant of the coach was the young man McAllister had noticed at Tully's the night before – the one somebody thought was somebody's nephew. Ham Stoppard, the bank teller, asked him sociably: 'Going beyond Caspar, sir?'

The young man smiled brightly and said: 'Chicago.'

The drummer said: 'What's your line, sir? If a man may ask.'

'Sure,' said the young man affably, 'I'm a journalist. I have been doing a number of pieces on the Wild West.'

The rancher chuckled at that. 'Ain't that just like a

goddam easterner?' he demanded. 'No offence, young feller. Wild West! Hell, there ain't nothing wild left about the West, boy. We're a sight more peaceable than the east. I'd rather walk across this territory any day of the week than cross a street in Chicago.'

The young man said: 'You could well be right, sir. But a man has to make a living, and if the readers say the West has to be wild, that's the way I make it.' He seemed remarkably unashamed.

Ham Stoppard laughed. 'If we had known,' he said, 'we would have had some of the boys fix a shoot-out in town for you. They would have liked that. I saw them do it once for one of those dime novelists and they sure had a lot of fun.'

The rancher entered into the spirit of the thing and said: 'Or we could have had an Indian attack. I reckon that would of gone down well, huh?'

The drummer suggested: 'Or a stage hold-up. That would have been capital.'

'Yes,' said the newspaperman, 'a hold-up would have been really something.'

'Too late now,' said the drummer regretfully.

Archly, the rancher said: 'We ain't at Caspar yet, boys,' and they all laughed and crossed their fingers.

The stage was stopped almost exactly halfway between Black Horse and Caspar. The hold-up men had picked a pretty spot just at the top of a steep gradient in the road before a bend, where the team would naturally be moving at no more than a walking pace.

The road agents were brutal, fast and efficient, three reasons why they had control of the situation from beginning to end. The first indication they gave of their presence was when the nearside leader dropped in the traces, shot through the head. That stopped the stage getting away, in the only certain way it could be stopped.

Next, three men appeared, two on one side and one on the other side of the trail. Each man held a revolver. Only one man spoke throughout the operation. He was a smallish man, dressed in a duster, like the other men, so that his clothes were concealed. A blue and white bandanna covered the lower part of his face. A broad-brimmed black hat was pulled low over his eyes. He spoke with a foreign accent.

'Throw down the strong-box.'

Without a word, Horry Wanlace and Wally Hunt climbed down from their seats and unstrapped the boot. They heaved the strong-box onto the trail. Horry looked as if he was ready to burst into tears.

The road agents' mouthpiece said: 'Cut the dead horse free and drive on.' The two men obeyed. Horry led the team round the body of the dead animal. The offside leader was awkward without his running companion, so Horry cut him loose too and tied him on behind. Then he and Wally climbed aboard and Horry drove on. It was no good their looking back, because they were around the bend in the trail and unable to see the road agents.

Horry said: 'My God, that does it, Wal. Don't it just do it?'

'It sure does it,' said Wally. 'Christ, I couldn't even get off a shot, Horry.'

'Sure you couldn't get off a shot,' said Horry. 'I got a dead horse. That's enough. I don't want a dead messenger too. The firm can't stand that kind of a loss.'

'That's a generous attitude, Horry,' Wally said, 'and it sure is appreciated.'

Inside the coach, the passengers were looking decidedly sober. The young man from Chicago said: 'We spoke too soon, all right.'

'Yeah,' said Ham Stoppard, 'we sure did. My God, the old man's going to play hell over this.'

The rancher said: 'We're still alive, ain't we? I regard that as a reason for rejoicing. What was in that strong-box, Ham?'

Stoppard shrugged. 'I don't have any idea.'

The drummer, who had produced a quart of bad but wonderfully powerful liquor which may or may not have claimed to be whiskey, offered the bottle around and said: 'It must have been mighty valuable.'

The young man from Chicago nodded in agreement. He was the only one on that stage who knew just how valuable.

3

Having his coach stopped and the strong-box taken just about broke up Horry Wanlace. Every man has his weak spot, and pride in his little stage line was Horry's. He did not go all to pieces, but he took it hard. One thing that he did not do was admit defeat. He took his stage on to Caspar, because that was what he had been hired to do and what was expected of him. Once in Caspar, he used the new telegraph wire to inform Sheriff McAllister of what had happened, just in case the sheriff could think of something smart to do, and Horry was damned if he could think of what else he could do. He had already made good his loss of one horse by picking up a fresh animal at his way-station between the hills and Caspar. Now he rested his team overnight at his stable in the town and slept on the whole problem. He was alert enough to take the names and addresses of the passengers on the stage.

When he woke the following morning, he was not a little surprised to find none other than Remington McAllister, maddeningly bright and cheerful as a cricket, sitting on the edge of his bed. Horry was never too bright and cheerful himself first thing of a morning. He snarled: 'You didn't waste any time.'

'A friend in need...' said McAllister. 'Tell me all you know about the hold-up. Every last detail, unimportant or not.'

Horry groaned and said: 'Before I even taste a cup of java?'

McAllister said: 'Get dressed. I reckon every baby needs a tit.'

Horry didn't think that too nice a thing to say, but he rose, slapped his face once with cold water, pulled on his clothes, stamped his feet into his boots and followed McAllister down into the hotel dining room. While he sipped his hot sweet coffee in deep disgust, he watched McAllister consume one large steak with onions and fried potatoes on the side and swallow three cups of coffee to his one. As he sipped, he talked. He gave McAllister credit for keeping silent until he was through talking.

Then McAllister said: 'I already had the newsman's name and paper from Stoppard, and I checked by wire with Pinkerton in Chicago. They owe me. There's nobody called William Bentley on the newspaper, and what's more he did not go on to Chicago. He walked off into the night from town in a southerly direction and was never seen again.'

'You don't mean that young feller–'

'Most likely. Horry, we never had a hyste in our neck of the woods before and this has to be the last. So we catch these men.'

'Just like that,' said Horry, not without scorn.

'First thing, I want to look at the tracks left by the road agents. I'll ride back with you to where you were stopped.' McAllister thought a moment.'You reckon the man who talked was a Mexican?'

'Sure.'

'You ever heard any other kind of a foreigner talk?'

'Sure I did. All sorts. Dutchmen, Frenchies and all the rest.'

'And you'd swear on your life this was a Mexican?'

'Not on my life, I wouldn't.'

Fifteen minutes later, Horry and Wally Hunt were up behind a team and Horry's whip was cracking. McAllister had Oscar tied behind the stage and he rode inside. The vehicle was carrying more passengers back to Black Horse than it had brought out. Sitting opposite McAllister was Ham Stoppard. He was still pretty upset by what had happened, for he considered that he had been mainly responsible for the strong-box. You could see him thinking to himself: 'I don't know what Mr J. Howard Lindholm is going to say about this.' He kept swallowing, and his adam's apple jumped up and down alarmingly.

On one side of the bank teller sat a cattleman, smelling of cows and leather. On the other side sat a young woman with downcast eyes and a face and figure that was apt to snap a man's eyes out of his head. McAllister thought it was a damn shame, with such a vision as that sitting opposite him, that he was riding no more than half way. She had dark brown hair, and under the duster which vainly tried to conceal her charms she wore a blue and white gingham cotton dress. Once, when a wheel hit a rock on the trail and the stage leapt like a living thing into the air and landed again with an almighty jolt, her eyes opened in alarm. They opened wide and gave McAllister the chance to see that they were of the purest cornflower blue and of quite breathtaking beauty. To add to their perfection, they were edged by lashes as dark as a raven's wing.

As if to counteract too much pulchritude in one place at the same time, providence had placed next to McAllister on his right what can only be described as a ripe-scented hill-nutty. In short, an aged prospector for gold, who smelled of many years presence in the company of burros and absence from the society of men. If his ancient body had looked upon water during the last five years, McAllister would have been amazed. To face the perils of the stage-journey and the hazards of the trail, this old number had seriously imbibed of hard liquor for the most part of the night before. His frequent belches perfumed the air of the interior of the vehicle.

As if to complement this denizen of distant gulches, on the left of McAllister there was a younger version of the same breed who had apparently slept for long periods with unhygienic goats. This fellow was as talkative as his old counterpart was silent, throwing pearls of boring wisdom to the world in general with a generosity that must have earned him many enemies along the trail.

Except for the young beauty on the seat facing him, McAllister was glad enough to dismount when Horry pulled in his harness-hating mustangs at the very spot where the bandits had robbed him of the strong-box the day before. Not, however, before McAllister had ascertained that the young lady who had so aroused his interest was one Miss Allison Disart who was travelling west to keep house for her uncle, Josiah Ramage.

Josiah Ramage? thought McAllister. Who in hell was Josiah Ramage? An inhabitant of Black Horse? If so, he could not place him – which was a failing on his part, because he thought he knew every last man, woman and child in Black Horse country.

When he got out of the stage, Ham Stoppard, Horry and the messenger joined him. Horry described what had happened and where the hold-up men had been placed. The varmints had been at the dead horse, McAllister noted, and there was little left of it. Ham Stoppard, not wishing to go back to Black Horse immediately (for which nobody could blame him) asked if he could stay with McAllister to aid him in his investigations. McAllister solemnly thanked him and refused his company.

'To tell you the truth, Ham,' he said, 'I could use you to better purpose in town. I expect to be in Black Horse by night and I would like to know exactly what was in the strong-box.'

'I guess that would be confidential,' said Ham.

McAllister said coldly: 'It'll be staying confidential. You'll be telling your sheriff, Ham, not publishing it in the *Courier*.' Ham climbed back into the stage, a little hurt, but he cheered up considerably when Miss Disart favoured him with a brilliant smile. Driver and messenger climbed back onto the box and Horry cracked his whip. McAllister tied Oscar to a tree at the side of the road and spent the next hour going over the sign that had been left in the locality.

At the end of that hour, he knew that there had been four men there. Four men and five horses. The fifth horse had been a powerful pack animal and it had borne away the strong-box. The man who had shot the lead stage horse had never appeared from cover, but had stayed out of sight, most likely with his rifle covering the crew and passengers. McAllister learned a few other facts.

The man who had done the talking had been below medium height and heavily-made. To compensate him for his lack of height, maybe, he had worn unusually high heels to his cowman's boots. Every man there had been well-mounted on shod horses. They had scattered in all directions immediately after the departure of the stage.

McAllister decided to follow the man who had done the talking, if only because he had led the pack horse. He did wonder if this was some kind of a bluff and hesitated for a moment, but he reckoned that the leader had been the talker and that the leader would want to keep the plunder with him. Leaders were like that. This leader had gone directly south along the line of the hills, hitting a good pace but not hurrying unduly. The tracks were not difficult to follow, even though the weather had been dry lately. But McAllister did not allow that to lull into a sense of easy success. He at once had the instinctive feeling that this man was smart and that if he had not wanted McAllister to follow him, it would not have been so easy. Sooner or later, McAllister knew, this man would lead him to a spot where the tracks could be lost.

A couple of hours later, he was proved right.

This did not please him. He wanted to move fast for many reasons, and this setback meant that there would be a long delay. If he picked up the fellow's sign this side of dusk, he would be surprised.

The place where he lost the tracks was at a watersmeet, a place where a number of mountain streams ran together on a silt flat, which meant that there was a great shallow lake of moving and faintly rippling water, strewn with rocks and a few great boulders. He may be forgiven, I think, for expressing his feelings in a few words which would have sent the more respectable ladies of the Black Horse sewing bee into vapours and fits. He knew that he could circle this water till dark without finding a set of tracks which would lead him away from it. Each departing horseman (if indeed they had met here) could ride off along the bed of one of the numerous streams which fed this stretch of water. His utter defeat had been as simple as kiss your hand.

Never one to accept defeat without at least a loud

bellyache, McAllister rode to a somewhat higher and drier point and surveyed the scene. The town of Black Horse lay roughly west of his present position. In between himself and the town were first the foothills, above which he was now poised, and the broad sweep of the valley.

It was possible, even probable, that one of these streams flowed through the hills and into the valley. It might even be that it flowed on across the valley and fed his own Howard Creek.

Now that was a thought.

Without leaving a trail, a man might work his way right across the valley to within rifleshot of the town. Some son-of-a-bitch could have robbed the stage, ridden over here, down into the valley and across to Black Horse. He might even at this minute be sitting in Tully's doing his brave best to enjoy Tully's foul whiskey.

That was a fantastic thought, and McAllister dismissed it. It did, however, return to him from time to time rather persistently.

He headed Oscar down towards the foothills. The bandits could have left the watershed singly or together. They could have gone in any number of directions and he could not have followed them all. So he would attempt to pick up the trail of one of them. If he could find just one of them, he would cajole, threaten, bribe or plain scare him into revealing his accomplices and the whereabouts of the strong-box or its contents. Besides that, for private and personal reasons, he wanted the man who had killed the horse. He just naturally hated a man who could kill a horse out of hand.

McAllister was still following the little creek down out of the foothills when night overtook him. He did not have any supplies with him beyond the pocketful of jerky he never failed to carry on any kind of trip. As he never supped on jerky when he could encase a steak, he pulled off his path and visited with Carl Shiner and his wife Betty. They ran a hundred head on a small hill ranch not more than a couple of miles off his course.

Carl had been one of the wild ones until he met up with a

dance-hall girl and offered to make an honest woman of her. He was still a mite wild, but there was no real harm in him in McAllister's opinion, whose idea of wildness may not have been the preacher's. Betty was a scrawny, wind- and sun-tanned woman of thirty or so, who rode, swore and drank like a man. Though maybe a little better than the average man. She claimed to keep her man on the straight-and-narrow – bearing in mind it was her idea of straight-and-narrow, which may not have been the same as the local sheriff's.

They ran a pretty good little outfit between them and were comparatively honest, though naturally they were not crazy enough to eat their own beef. When they had welcomed McAllister, offered him a drink and sat him down to his favourite bait – a large steak with onions and potatoes fried – he wondered what brand the steak had worn when it was walking the Black Horse hills.

Though he thought it improbable that Shiner or his wife could help him, he mentioned the mission which had taken him to Caspar and into the foothills. They showed interest. It even passed through McAllister's mind that Shiner himself may have been one of the road agents, working on the assumption that to a lawman all men are suspect and others, by their very nature, more suspect than others.

Betty said: 'Rem, there was a feller that rid down the creek bed late afternoon yesterday. Our creek. I was up on the hill turning back a maverick that I thought might as well carry our brand.'

'Did you remember what he looked like, Betty?'

'I had my hands full of this beef, Rem. I reckon I just saw a man on a horse.'

'But you remember the horse?'

'Oh, sure, I remember the horse. Whoever forgot a horse?' That was a Westerner all over. Men were recognised for miles off from the horses they rode, when the rider's details were indistinguishable.

'Tell me all you can remember about the horse.'

'Fancy. A real fancy horse. One colour. Sorrel. A white stocking some place and a full-face blaze. California rig. And a how-d'you-call-it on its lines. You know what I mean, Rem. The lines're kind of joined together like an eastern rein.'

'With a romal?'

'I reckon.'

'The horse sounds like a thoroughbred.'

'As near as I ever seen one.'

'Where was this man headed?'

'Howard Creek. Maybe your place. Maybe town. Going in that direction.'

She screwed up her thin and leathery face in distaste. She said: 'I can't abide a man that'd shoot a horse.' Maybe she was telling the truth at that.

McAllister lay down in their barn alongside his horse and slept snug and well. In the morning, he ate for breakfast the same menu he had consumed for supper, thanked them courteously and went on his way. He did not fool around looking for tracks but rode home, letting Oscar stretch himself out across the valley before the sun rose high enough to make it too hot to run a horse that way. He reached home in the middle of the morning. Mose Copley was at work in the smithy and his boy, Lige, was gentling a colt in the round pen. They stopped work to hear his news. In response to McAllister's question, both replied that they had seen no strangers. Lige, however, said that he had gone out to take a look at the horses around midnight and heard a man come along the valley road and head in for town. He was not hurrying. Now he came to think of it, he thought he heard two horses together.

'Was he maybe leading a pack horse?'

'Maybe.'

McAllister unsaddled the gelding and threw his hull on his mare, Sally. He threw Oscar into the starve-out and said he was going on into town.

'What do you reckon was in that strong box?' Mose Copley wanted to know.

'I'm asking myself the same question. Maybe J. Howard Lindholm could tell me. And maybe he couldn't. We'll see.'

4

Josiah Ramage was known from Taos to the Dalles as Whiskey Joe, not so much because he was a boozer (which occasionally he was on an impressive scale), but because he swore that whiskey was the elixir of life. Inside and out, he reckoned and frequently announced, it was beneficial to man. It cured fever, ague, smallpox, cowardice, belly-ache, healed wounds, bites, stings and ulcers. Nothing as precious as whiskey had ever been revealed to man by divine providence. That his real name was Josiah Ramage was unknown to all mankind with the exception of J. Howard Lindholm, the owner of the Black Horse National Bank.

The revelation was made to Lindholm behind closed doors when Joe had sworn the banker to the strictest confidence, that he was most likely the richest man in the territory. Maybe in the whole of the West. Possibly in the whole world.

'Is that so?' Lindholm enquired politely but in complete and utter disbelief. He should not be blamed for this doubt. Nobody seeing this disreputable figure standing in front of him would have considered that any wealth belonged to this apparent beggar, dressed in his broken boots and ragged clothes, teeth missing, his look hangdog, his eyes red-rimmed and rheumy, his nose that of a dedicated drinker.

The man could have been any age ranging from forty to eighty. His face was rather like that of a pickled nut. A fair wind should have been enough to carry him off his feet. A light cough should have floored him and a mild slap on the back should have knocked him unconscious. His hair consisted of a few grey wisps above each ear. His massive hog-leg of a gun weighed him down disastrously on his left side. Anybody viewing him could rest assured that he had no more courage than a prairie dog and as much tenacity as a mouse.

In much of this, of course, the world misjudged him. Whiskey Joe was a resourceful, iron-nerved, resilient and tough old hill-nutty. He had braved all weathers, Indian threats, claim jumpers, thieves and even the law in his unrelenting search for gold. He claimed that he had found, and lost, at least two fortunes before this, but nobody believed him. This third fortune, he informed the banker, was not going to be so easily parted with.

'I've made my pile, Lindholm,' he said, 'and the devil himself ain't going to part me from it. That's where you come in. Act smart and you'll earn yourself a handsome fee. I have with me at this very minute something in the region of one hundred thousand dollars' worth of gold.'

Lindholm chuckled in a kindly and understanding way. 'My dear Joe,' he said, 'I am willing to believe you have gold. But one hundred thousand dollars' worth is a considerable amount. I see no sign of it.'

Joe looked at him pityingly. 'Jesus Christ,' he said, 'don't you go getting sassy with me, young feller. You buckle to and do like I say or I'll take my business some place else. The money's on my burros out on the street, ain't it?'

Ham Stoppard was recruited to carry the gold into the office, gunnysack by gunnysack. Lindholm took the opportunity to whisper to his teller: 'The old fool has finally taken leave of his senses. These sacks are full of sand. They have to be. Humour him and we'll get rid of him as soon as we can.'

When the sacks were piled on the office floor, Joe dismissed Ham Stoppard and opened a sack for Lindholm. I do not have to tell you, of course, that the sacks held gold. Each and every one of them. Some gold-dust, some nuggets which Lindholm could see would assay a high percentage of the precious metal. It was then that J. Howard Lindholm began to shake.

'My God,' he said, gazing at the prospector in awe, 'my

God, it's true.' He sat down because his legs failed him. He mopped his sweating brow. 'My God, can it really be true?' He had handled money and gold all his life, but he had never experienced anything like this.

His first thought was that Stoppard should never have witnessed the sacks being brought into the office.

He said to Joe: 'This is terrible. I mean wonderfully terrible, Joe. This must be guarded night and day.'

Joe said: 'Like I said, nobody must know about this but the two of us.'

'Stoppard already knows.'

'Can you trust him?'

'He's too simple to be anything but honest.' Even as he spoke Lindholm knew that he should not have said that. Whiskey Joe shot him an uneasy glance. 'All right,' he said, 'if you say so. But he got to be sworn. Like a deputy, on the Good Book. Hear?'

'Certainly, certainly,' said Lindholm and opened the door to call Ham in. Ham came in and his adam's apple went wild when he heard that he had toted real, genuine, actual gold, when all he thought he had toted was sand. Emulating his boss, he seemed to want to repeat himself a good deal. He said over and over: 'Oh, my stars. Oh, my stars, Mr Lindholm, sir.' He swore his oath with a gravity usually reserved for the marriage ceremony or the swearing of allegiance to the president. That done, he informed both his boss and old Whiskey Joe that he would guard the gold with his very life. And, when they took a good look at him, they knew that he meant it. He was a man who liked to devote himself to a cause.

The upshot of all this was that Mr Lindholm put as much of the gold as he could squeeze into his safe. The rest was stacked in a corner under papers and ledgers. He gave old Joe an advance of a few hundred dollars, and the prospector wandered off into town to prepare himself for affluence and life in civilisation – twin shocks which had seen the end of better men than he. However, he seemed happily unaware of this possible fate, bought himself a suit a size or two too large for him at Levy's store, then carried it down the street to

Cyril Heliopolous, the Greek barber, where he placed a mammoth order for a shave, a haircut and a bath. Seeing himself occupied for the remainder of the day, Cyril put up his CLOSED sign and got to work.

The result of Cyril's skill with clippers and scissors and razor, Joe's prolonged immersion in the hot tub, and the donning of the new clothes, worked a transformation in the old gold-hunter which was truly miraculous. At the tail-end of the day, there emerged from the Greek's a neatly dressed, distinguished-looking man of rather frail appearance, who looked out upon the world with a kind of mild wonder. His too-large clothes added somehow to the appearance of frailty. He might have been a retiring senator or a visiting professor.

He bought himself a ten cent cigar, lit up and parked himself on a bench outside Tully's which was the meeting place of the male section of the town. It took some time for the inmates of Tully's to recognise him. When they did so, they expressed untold wonder, they exclaimed, they bade others to come and look – seeing was almost believing.

'Joe,' said one, 'you must of struck it rich.'

The old man cackled a little. 'No such luck,' he declared. 'Brother of mine in Chicago passed away, God rest his soul. Made his money in sausages. Left his sausages to his eldest son. Bequeathed me a tidy sum to give me warmth and comfort in my last days.'

The crowd seemed to accept this story. One or two even bought Joe a drink on it. Joe, with the new-born caution of a rich man, did not shout for drinks all round. Not any more. Little wealth may be spent wildly; great wealth only with caution.

At last, Joe took himself along to the bank again, to find young Ham sitting over his gold with a loaded revolver on the table beside him. Lindholm was sitting behind his desk, dreaming of all the wonderful things which gold could buy.

Joe had made up his mind what he wanted to do with his gold. With his new confidence, he gave orders which, as a rich man, he expected to be carried out. Lindholm would obtain a strong-box, and it should go out under strict security to Caspar and thence to Chicago to one of the main banks. Lindholm did a rough and rapid estimate of how much gold they could get into a strong-box, and gladly assented.

'You're wise, Joe,' he said. 'Don't put all your eggs in one basket. Or in one strong-box – ha! ha! ha! One of my strong-boxes will take about one third of it. The rest, I feel sure, we could invest wisely here ourselves. What do you say to that?'

'I say "maybe",' said Joe, cocking a rheumy eye at him. 'I want the gold in the strong-box to go out on the next stage, hear? Under suitable guard.'

'Of course, of course. Anything you say, Joe.'

'I'll want a house here in town,' said Joe. 'I am expecting my niece in the next few days and I want a suitable home for her. She will look out for me from here on in.' That was the first they had heard of a niece, and they wondered if the old fool was making her up.

'What's your limit on the cost of a house?' the banker asked.

'Limit?' said Joe, in surprise and disgust, 'there ain't no limits on anything I want from this minute. You don't think this piddling little amount of gold is all I have, do you?'

They gazed at him in awe as he tramped from the bank.

'My stars,' said Ham Stoppard.

'I do declare,' Lindholm declared, 'that my mind is in a whirl.' In a whirl or not, it was most likely from that very moment that his mind began to scheme. This was a chance, after all, which did not come to a man usually in one lifetime.

5

There was a man sitting in McAllister's office when he walked in. The sheriff's mind was still on the man he had followed, or thought he had followed, across the valley.

When the man in the brown suit sitting in front of his desk turned and said: 'Morning, sheriff,' McAllister only knew that the voice was vaguely familiar and that the man was not. Which was perhaps a minor circumstance, but nonetheless a puzzling one.

'Morning,' said McAllister. 'What can I do for you?'

'Find my gold.'

McAllister sat behind his desk and took a long hard look at his visitor. 'Good God,' he said finally, 'it's Whiskey Joe.'

'Josiah Ramage now.'

'So you're Josiah Ramage!'

'You bet, and it was my gold that was taken off the Caspar stage. I'm offering a re-ward. One thousand dollars.'

'Ah,' said McAllister with some satisfaction, 'that's what I like to hear.'

'Everybody likes to hear money.'

'And that was your niece who came in on the stage.'

'The same. And you keep your horny eyes off her, young feller. She's here to keep house for her old uncle, not fool around with the local rams.'

'I've been out looking for sign, Joe.'

'Any luck?'

'No.'

'Maybe the thousand dollars will encourage you to further efforts.'

'Joe, don't put up the money as a reward. Let me have it to draw on when I need it for work on this case. I'm more or less alone on the job and I could do with some help.'

That wary eye was cocked again.

But Joe knew McAllister and he knew his reputation. He thought about it, then said: 'Leave the reward as it stands. I've enough left to back you for expenses.'

'You won't regret it.'

'I'd best not.'

Then McAllister questioned him and ended up with the following information. Nobody, so far as Joe knew, had any idea where the source of the gold was. The strike was nowhere nearly played out and there was plenty more where the gold in the bank came from. Who knew that? Joe did, and nobody else. Hadn't he mentioned it to a soul? Yes, he had. He'd told Lindholm and Stoppard.

'From here on, Joe, you don't tell anybody anything. Just keep your mouth shut tight. And don't go around without a gun.'

Joe looked a little alarmed. McAllister explained: 'Maybe they plan to take all the gold from you, Joe. When that's done, they'll be greedy and they'll want the rest. You'll see. The only way to get information about your claim is to squeeze it out of you.'

Joe said: 'I didn't think of that. Hell, I can see the fun of being rich can go kind of sour.'

McAllister said: 'Most everything goes sour when men get greedy.' Where could he find Joe if he wanted him? Joe proudly told him that he had bought a nice house on the north end of Morrow, right on the edge of town, looking out over the valley.

'Come around and have dinner with me one night, Rem,' said the old man. 'You might find it amusing. I keep a good cellar.'

'A good what?' said McAllister.

'Oh,' Joe said airily, 'a rich man has to be fussy about his wines.'

He could not better that line, so he made his exit onto the street and left McAllister to gaze after him.

McAllister got up and walked to the bank. Ham Stoppard was not at his usual place behind the counter. Another clerk told McAllister that the teller was not available.

'Where is he?'

'In Mr Lindholm's office.'

McAllister stepped to the inner office door, knocked and turned the handle. The door was locked. From inside a voice demanded to know who he was. He replied and, after some mumbled conversation inside, the door opened. He stepped inside and the door was immediately locked behind him. Ham Stoppard sat, gun in hand. He was trying to look grim and dangerous, but failed. Instead, he looked like a young bank teller with the belly-ache.

'McAllister,' said the banker, 'I'm sure I do not have to tell you that the robbery of this gold is intolerable.'

'Gold,' said McAllister, 'what gold?'

'The gold on the stage, of course.'

'I wasn't told there was gold on the stage,' said McAllister. He rounded slowly on Stoppard, incredulity in his eyes. 'You don't mean to tell me, Ham, that you knew there was gold in that strong-box all the time?'

'I was under orders to keep the information to myself,' said Ham manfully, his adam's apple dancing frantically.

'Whose orders?'

'Mr Lindholm's, of course.'

McAllister said softly: 'You mean that Mr Lindholm is above the law, Ham?' And the sheriff slowly turned his gaze to the banker, who bristled a little and said: 'I have to protect my clients.'

McAllister said: 'This one didn't get protected too well. In future, Mr Lindholm, we shall know about gold shipments and we shall make sure that they are adequately guarded.'

'There has never been a robbery of this kind around here before.'

McAllister jerked his head in the direction of the safe and said: 'But there'll be another, I shouldn't wonder, with that safe stuffed tight as it is. We'll ship that on the next stage, Mr Lindholm.'

The banker showed his panic for just a small fraction of a second. 'Would that be wise?'

'A damn sight wiser than leaving it here.'

McAllister let himself out of the room. He walked along Main and turned right at the intersection into Morrow. At the bottom of Morrow, sure enough, there stood Whiskey Joe's newly-purchased house: a handsome frame building with a neat white picket fence around it and a stout shed for a buggy to the rear. His knock on the street door was answered by the girl from the stage, as McAllister hoped and expected.

Her eyes were as blue as ever and they quite bowled him over. He thought that a man of his age being bowled over by a girl young enough to be his daughter (well, nearly young enough) was slightly ridiculous. But he was bowled over just the same.

She remembered him from the stage and said nicely: 'Come in, sheriff.' He took off his hat and followed her into the house. She sat him on the gallery at the rear of the building, overlooking the valley, and there she served him cold lemonade.

'I really came to see Joe,' he said. 'But I'd rather talk to you.'

She dimpled, and he liked that. He wondered if she was as well-mannered and gentle as she looked, all through and through, that is. Nobody, surely, could be all that well-mannered and gentle.

'I'd like to talk to you about Joe. We can talk about the weather, and you, and the latest fashions in Chicago, but we have to settle for old Joe. You know he's a rich man, now?'

'Yes, I know.' Her voice was little more than a whisper.

'Somebody held the stage up and took his gold. Did he tell you that?'

'Yes.'

'There's more gold, and somebody could be after that, too. I'm not trying to scare you, but I have to think of the old man. You see that?'

'Clearly.'

'Good. Now, I think it would be a good idea for you to talk Uncle Joe into taking you to Chicago for a few months.

Time enough for me to clear this business up. How does that sound to you? Just I don't want him hurt. He's made his pile after wasting a life looking for it.'

'I understand you perfectly, Mr McAllister. I'll do my best, but I can't promise anything. Old men can be very obstinate.'

'So can young women.'

She laughed, and he had never heard a laugh quite like it. She became completely the young girl, untouched by life. He could not believe the evidence of his eyes.

'May a man ask what you did for a living in Chicago, ma'am, or don't you have to work?'

She looked at him directly, those blue eyes large and wide. His experience told him that this kind of a woman gave you that kind of a look when she was about to tell you the lie of the year.

'I took in washing with my mother,' she said. When his eyes showed their disbelief, she held out her hands and proved her statement.

'So having a rich uncle,' said McAllister, 'is like a dream coming true.'

'However unpleasant the uncle,' she said, 'it would be better than washing other people's dirty linen. But, thank God, this one is a nice old man.'

He stood up and said: 'Ma'am, I misjudged you.'

'Catch the thieves, Mr McAllister,' she said, 'for my sake as well as Uncle Joe's.'

McAllister smiled and said: 'Ma'am, I intend to do that.'

As he walked away from the house, he was modest enough to wonder how the hell he *would* do it.

6

A man is dealt a hand of cards with which to play out and gamble on the game of his life. Some are strong, some weak, but the kind of hand you hold does not necessarily indicate how a man may make out in life.

J. Howard Lindholm had been dealt a pretty good hand, one way and another. One good card was his luck. He had the luck of the devil. And, when I come to think of it, that's not a bad way of putting it. There was something of the devil about him.

His strongest card, of course, was his appearance. This was rather suggestive of a cuddly bear. No man looking like that, you would have thought, could possess guile, let alone cunning. To look so slightly ridiculous somehow did not also permit him to be dangerous. He looked a gentle and rather ineffectual man, which was probably his best disguise of all. It was his sheer inconsequence which was his hole card. Nobody could take him really seriously.

Not that he was bad at business. When it came to business, cattlemen said, 'old J. Howard was all there and no mistake.' He understood interest and percentages, money having confidence in itself, the difference between a gamble and an investment. Since coming to Black Horse some two years before, he had given a number of men good advice and strengthened the financial position of one or two quite powerful men among the cattle kings.

Nobody guessed that J. Howard Lindholm had been biding his time. While he drank tea in polite parlours, chatted amiably to the milliner on Main, passed the time of day with the preacher and doffed his hat with grave and slightly comical courtesy to the hardware store owner's wife.

He bided his time. Just as he had done in Plainton, Illinois. He had had a beard then, and been slightly overweight. He had given way in his former years to weaknesses of the flesh. They were mostly conquered now. He had lost thirty pounds without much suffering, shaved his face and changed his name. He made it look as though he had fled to New York and thence to South America, but in fact he came West with the money from the safe of the bank that employed him as a teller. He had used the money wisely and maybe a little unscrupulously for some ten years in various towns of the West, but had done nothing further to attract the attention of law officers. He had loaned it at a high return, staked prospectors, that kind of thing. In ten years he had made enough capital to establish himself as a banker in a community such as Black Horse. In the two years since he came here, he had proven himself a solid man. Folks trusted him. He showed financial kindness to a few hard-pressed but powerful men who found themselves short of a little ready cash.

He had, for example, nonchalantly handed a thousand dollars to the rancher Stoke Parlby and never asked for a note in return. 'Good heavens, Stoke,' he had said, 'I don't do this as a banker, but as a friend. If a friend can't help another . . . ' Parlby invariably said when Lindholm's name came up in conversation: 'By God, there's a man in a million.'

How right he was.

Lindholm's card that beat all other cards, of course, was his self-control. He could be decisive and ruthless, but that ruthlessness was always under iron control. It was just nice to know that it was there, like a hideway gun in a vest pocket, to be exploded lethally in a man's face when it was needed. When necessary, Lindholm could be utterly devoid of mercy or any other human feeling.

All men have weaknesses, however, and in this the banker was no different from other men. His weakness, as with most men who live by deception, was his vanity. He knew it, and he tried to guard against it. But how difficult to deny that he was smarter than almost anybody he had ever met. Who was clever enough to keep his true self carefully and successfully hidden from the world?

He stood at the window of the bank now and glanced up and down the street, feeling so powerful by the coup he had pulled off that it was as if he could reach out and take the town in the palm of his hand. He was glad that his face was turned away from that simple fool Ham Stoppard, and the boy could not see the expression on his face. His mind considered the teller. He must make a small gesture or two to the boy. Show some appreciation for his extra duty guarding the gold.

Lindholm turned from the window and said: 'Ham, old chap, I want to tell you that the bank is grateful for all the extra time you have put in lately. Very commendable, and you shall not lose by it. We shall make a nice little profit from the handling of this fortune and the bank will be happy to share a little of it with you. What about a hundred dollars?'

Ham stared at him in amazement. His adam's apple leapt.

'A hundred dollars? Oh, Mr Lindholm, you mean you're not still mad at me for losing that strong-box?'

'Mad at you? Good grief, boy, what could you do against four dangerous armed men? I never expected you to lay down your life for a dross of gold. A man's life is worth more than that. You are a valued employee of this establishment. No, I do not think a hundred dollars is too much to pay for unshakable loyalty.

'I'm very grateful, sir.'

'Not at all, my boy. Now, I intend to have a truckle bed brought in here for you so that you may sleep here in comfort at night. How does that sound?'

'Splendid, Mr Lindholm.'

'Excellent, excellent. I'm going out now. Lock the door behind me.' He gave Ham a cuddly smile and went out into the bright sunlight of Main Street. As he walked past Tully's, there was a man standing on the sidewalk outside building a smoke. He noticed that the man wore his bandanna pulled tight against the throat, but with the cloth no more than half-secured by a single turn. That was the signal. Lindholm walked on past and, in spite of his self-control, he could not prevent the swoop of sudden excitement in the pit of his stomach.

So it was all done. The gold was clear of the country. All was secure. Now for the next move. He reached the intersection and turned right down Morrow. Right at the bottom of the street, he could see Josiah Ramage's new house. Lindholm smiled to himself. Now that the gold was safe, he felt flushed with new strength and confidence. It was a good feeling and he experienced a surge of happiness. What a wonderful world he lived in. How lucky he was to be so successful and to have been endowed with such talent.

Now, now, Lindholm, he told himself. Modesty at all times. Anything else could lead to over-confidence, and that could be fatal.

His knock on the Ramage street door was answered by Miss Allison Disart, a fact which pleased J. Howard immensely, for nobody liked a fine-looking woman more than he did. Her uncle had introduced him to her on the street the day before, and he had been struck by her beauty and attractions. Since the meeting, his thoughts had once or twice returned to her. He found that each time they did so they were a little warmer than the last, and that his imagination grew a little more colourful. By jingo, he thought, maybe she was a young woman who found slightly more mature men attractive. She certainly looked intelligent enough.

Her uncle, she told him now, was on the rear gallery, and she led the way down the hall. Walking behind her, he had a chance to inspect her from where her dark hair curled on her creamy neck, to the slender waist and the irresistible swell of her fine hips. She was, as the boys at Tully's would say, a hell of a lot of woman.

Whiskey Joe was on the back porch, jacket off, vest unbuttoned and booted feet up on the rail. As a rich man he could greet the banker casually, and he promptly did so.

'Howdy, Lindholm. Hot ain't it? Park yourself someplace. Ally, honey, just you make yourself scarce now. Dry old business stuff ain't for pretty girls to bother their heads with.'

She went into the house.

'A remarkably fine-looking young lady, Joe, if I may say so,' said Lindholm.

Joe said: 'Now you keep your mind on business, J. Howard, and off that gal. You're old enough to be her daddy.'

'My dear Joe, I assure you –'

'Assure me nothing, man. You're male and over fourteen, ain't you? Hell, take that look off your face. I'm only joshing. Set. Drink some of that goddamn lemonade I'm rotting my guts with.'

The banker poured a glass of lemonade and sipped it. He leaned forward and spoke in low tones. Some secrecy was called for, he felt, even out here.

'Joe, I've been thinking about all this gold.'

'I never stop. Lovely, ain't it?'

'Seriously, I have an uneasy feeling. The gold was taken off the stage. It was done efficiently. How many efficient road agents have you and I ever heard of? Most of them are bungling amateurs. These boys knew their business. If they've gone for one shipment, what's to stop them going for another?'

'I'd expect that. But they won't get it. McAllister'll ride shotgun. I'll hire other guards. Nobody don't take gold off old Joe twice. My word on it.'

'We must think further than that, Joe.' Lindholm was earnest, he was impressive. He used his slightly hesitant manner, denoting a modest man, but one who knew what he was talking about.

'As your business adviser –'

'Say,' said Joe, looking at him with delight on his wrinkled face, 'is that what you are? Hell, I like the sound of that. Sure, a millionaire has to have a business adviser, don't he?'

'Seriously, Joe, with your best interests at heart, I think that we should give consideration to the rest of the gold.'

'Young Ham's guarding that.'

'I mean the gold you haven't brought out yet.'

Joe took his feet down from the rail and considered Lindholm soberly. 'I ain't telling you where it's at, if that's what you're driving at.'

'No, no, no – perish the thought. What I'm saying is that if these men are organised and they can't get at the gold you're shipping out on the stage, they're going to start thinking.'

'They're going to pack up their traps and clear out.'

'With more gold untouched in the hills somewhere?'

Joe was still. 'What's on your mind?'

'On my mind, I have the idea of well-organised, patient thieves. Men who are smart enough to wait. Sooner or later, you will go to that gold. If you go to it, they can. No matter what you do, a good tracker can follow – and you know it.'

'Go ahead.'

'I merely have an idea that it might be wise for us to organise too.'

'What do you mean?'

'If there's enough gold in your mine to finance it, we should obtain the necessary machinery – crushers and that kind of thing – bring in labourers, work the mine to its full capacity. Clean up, Joe, once and for all. Get the whole thing on a sound business footing. Maybe you think it isn't worth it.'

'Worth it! Jesus, Lindholm, I struck Eldorado. I could finance anything I damn well please.'

'Well then . . . '

'I dunno. What's so wrong with the way I'm playing it now? I'm rich enough, ain't I?'

'You've worked hard all your life, Joe. Now's the time to take it easy. Hire the work done.'

'It sure is a thought,' said the old man. 'But the whole world will know then.'

'The world's got to learn sooner or later.'

'I druther it was later.'

'But you could be in real danger, Joe.' Lindholm played his hand carefully, not pushing too hard with his voice. 'I mean physical danger. If these men ever got their hands on you in an attempt to discover where the gold is . . . '

'Now you're letting your imagination run away with you, J. Howard,' Joe said. 'This is Black Horse. We have law and order here. Nobody ain't going to threaten me.'

Lindholm rose. 'All right. I'm not trying to pressure you. I just leave you with the idea so you can think on it. There's your niece to consider now, too. Thanks for the lemonade.'

Joe made a face. 'I'll think about it.'

Lindholm walked back into the house. He hoped he would see the girl again, but he did not – and found himself more disappointed than he thought possible.

7

As he paced down Morrow and turned into Main, sweating somewhat more than a little, a refrain kept going through his head: *McAllister will ride on the stage. McAllister will ride on the stage.*

He knew that would mean a fight if the stage was attacked. Men would be killed. And that was not something he wanted. Not that he objected morally to a man or two being killed. He merely felt that murder was distasteful and, in most cases, foolish. It wanted only for one of his road agent colleagues to be killed and the whole operation would turn sour. Those four men were in it for the profit, not to exchange shots with an over-enthusiastic lawman. Goddam that McAllister to hell.

Just the same, he hated to have a whole strong-box of gold lost to him.

Was that a sign of weakness in him? Had he become greedy? Maybe it would be wise to allow the stage line to get the next consignment through safely.

Yes, he decided, he would do that. There must not be a breath of suspicion against him.

Now, another question came into his head to plague him. How long could he keep the road agents in the country with safety? They were all good men. They all knew their business. But they now had a large amount of gold in their possession and at least one of them must be at this very moment tempted to go out and spend some of it. There was always one such in a gang.

Walking towards him came Charlie Stellino. Charlie did not have much going for him in J. Howard Lindholm's eyes. First, he was a friend of McAllister and Mark Tully. Second, he had no respect for money. Third, he had no respect. Period. He was a no-good wastrel who fooled around with a few cows and called himself a cattleman, living, if gossip was right (and gossip usually was right over such things) on other men's beef. It was a scandal that the sheriff should be in cahoots with such riff-raff. Charlie Stellino could do McAllister's reputation no good and one day he would bring McAllister down.

Just as Charlie approached him, Lindholm saw, emerging from a rooming house, a decrepit figure which the banker at once recognised as belonging to a prospector who had come into town on the same stage as Allison Disart. Charlie halted, cocked an eye at Lindholm and pointed to the prospector.

'He smells gold, Lindholm,' Charlie said. 'That baby don't go nowhere where there ain't gold.'

'Well,' said Lindholm stiffly, 'there's no gold around here, Stellino. That's a well-known fact.'

'I heard different,' said the cowman.

Alarm blossomed in Lindholm. 'You heard talk of gold?' he said, trying to keep his sudden disquiet from his voice.

'Sure did. Can't recollect where, but I sure heard it.'

'Do you mean actually in Black Horse country?'

'I reckon so.'

'You know what I say to that, Stellino?'

'No. What do you say to that, Lindholm?'

‘I say “Stuff and nonsense, sir.”’ And with that he went on past the cowman.

Stellino grinned and shrugged. He wondered: Maybe that strong-box the town had seen Lindholm put on the stage...

The banker consulted the gold hunter he kept in his right-hand vest pocket. The time reminded him that he must hurry. He arrived at his office, sweating noticeably. He found also that he was irritable; something which he could not afford. He must play his part perfectly now and through the near future. He must not spoil his own grand plan by a silly little mistake, by giving offence to anybody. He tapped on his office door and was challenged by Ham. Thank God, he thought, for fools like Ham.

When he walked into the office and Ham locked the door behind him, the banker saw that his teller held the gun in his hand.

‘Ham,’ he said, ‘squeezing his voice into a kindly shape, ‘take a spell. You’ve been long enough incarcerated in this room. Go breathe some fresh air for an hour, take a tub and smoke a cigar. I’ll mind the store, as they say.’

Ham expressed his appreciation at the banker’s concern. He gave the impression of being a humble man truly grateful for the fate which had brought him into the service of so considerate a man.

He had not been gone from the bank for more than five minutes when the other teller tapped on the door and announced to Lindholm that there was a Mr Stevenson to see him.

Lindholm opened the door to receive his visitor, saying: ‘Why, Mr Stevenson, how good to see you, sir. Come in, come in.’

The newcomer was a man of some presence. The teller returned to his counter under the impression that he had been privileged to see a man of substance, one of those divine creatures who form and motivate the actions and affairs of lesser men.

Inside the office, Lindholm waved the visitor to a chair and inspected him with the greatest care. He saw a tall, personable man, possessed of a distinguished air, a strong and natural character and a physical well-being and fitness beyond the average. His features, while not exactly handsome, were imposing, very nearly noble, but too worldly and too full of common good-humour for that. It was the face of a man who had lived, possibly a little too thoroughly and even maybe hectically. He had, one suspected, frequently looked on the wine while it was red and the women who were willing.

When the stranger spoke, it was in a well-modulated and pleasant voice, but with enough rough corners and Yankee drawls to make it a voice of character. 'How private are we here?'

'The room is to all practical purposes sound-proof. Speak in a natural tone and nobody outside will hear you.'

'Good. Now, let's not waste time. I thought the job the other day went well.'

'Excellent,' said Lindholm. 'Capital. Bully.'

'So, do you deem it wise to give a repeat performance?'

'The second consignment is due out on tomorrow's stage.'

Stevenson smiled easily. 'Do we gather ye rosebuds while we may? Or do we accept that discretion is the better part of valour? In short, do we do a hyste or don't we?'

'I confess that I'm still debating,' said Lindholm. 'I'm tempted to run a dummy tomorrow and plead that I thought there would be a second hold-up. It would establish me as being cautious on Joe's behalf.'

'Something to be said for that. I and the boys are in no hurry. We all realise the size of this caper. None of us would want to spoil it with undue haste or inordinate greed.'

'Good to hear you say that. There's something else against your hitting the stage tomorrow. If you do so, there could be bloodshed. The last thing we want is that kind of thing. I think you would agree.'

'Every time, but why do you think –'

'McAllister's riding shotgun.'

There was silence in the room. Stevenson raised his eyebrows.

'McAllister!' He pondered the information. 'Isn't it a little unusual for a sheriff?'

'It's a fact and we have to face it.'

Stevenson said: 'J. Howard, let me think about this. Just give me a minute. No more.'

'Go ahead.'

The tall man rose and walked to the window and gazed up and down Main, much as Lindholm did when he stood there. The banker watched the man, noting the excellent cut of the pale grey clawhammer coat, the first-class hang of the matching pants. Elegant was the word.

Finally, Stevenson turned from the window. He returned to his seat and carelessly threw one leg over the other, showing off the fine Mexican boots under the pants' cuffs.

'J. Howard,' he said, 'there's a whole lot more in this than the gold we have and the gold you have here in this office. Let's play this as calmly as we know how. Let's string McAllister along. No matter if we lose a little gold in the short-term. I suggest that you ship real gold out with McAllister and that it gets through safely to Caspar, to Chicago, wherever it's intended. Then you make a dummy run which we may or may not stop. But certainly, when you send the next genuine consignment, we grab it. Not on the trail, but in Caspar itself.'

Lindholm gazed at him with admiration and sincere pleasure.

'Stevenson,' he said, 'you're a man after my own heart. It was a happy day when we agreed to do business together.'

'Nice to hear it.'

8

Small communities need few policemen not so much because they are small, but because every man is his own policeman. A stranger stands out like a sore thumb, as you might say. Equally, if a local man commits a crime, somebody is bound to recognise him.

So it was that McAllister knew that there were two strangers in town and had been since the day after the stage hold-up. He knew their names and where they were staying. One was Henry Holst Stevenson and he was staying, as might be expected, at the Grand Union Hotel. The other was a man named Madders, who paid rent on a nightly bed at Ma Shane's on the new-grown street of Mullaly, which ran parallel to and a block west of Morrow. It already had a shabby and shady look about it. Here was the street where the deadfalls naturally found themselves. If the area went on growing, the town committe men said, they would be hiring themselves a policeman. Madders had drifted into the respectable part of town to take a drink or three at Tully's. No connection between Stevenson and Madders had been noticed by anybody.

From his observation point at his office window, McAllister saw Stevenson go into the bank. A short while later, he saw the man at the window of Lindholm's office, looking up and down the street much as the banker did. McAllister did not miss the fact that Ham Stoppard vacated the office while Stevenson was there.

Charlie Stellino walked into the office and McAllister said: 'You must of known I wanted to see you.'

Charlie said: 'I must of known your whiskey, while being fit for nothing, is a sight better than the rot-gut sold by our friend Tully. Produce it, McAllister, before you get a single civil word from me.'

McAllister opened a drawer and produced a bottle. While Charlie made it gurgle its sweet tune, McAllister said: 'I need a deputy for a while.'

The melody stopped. Stellino eyed him balefully and without affection. 'Do you no damn good looking at me.'

'Pays one-twenty a month.'

'I'm your man.'

'You ride shotgun on the stage with me tomorrow.'

'I reject the badge. I spurn one-twenty a month. Who likes to get shot at?'

McAllister said: 'You're already committed. Too late to draw back.'

Charlie took a long pull and McAllister took the bottle from him, saying: 'One more pull at that and it'll be deducted from your wages.'

Charlie sat down and stared at McAllister. 'I ain't deef you know. I heard about the hold-up. That time they killed a horse. A man that can do a dirty low-down thing like killing a horse ain't going to stop at knocking off a man. Or can you tell me different?'

'A whole lot different. Five'll get you ten there won't be any hold-up.'

Charlie sat quietly there, thinking. He looked like a half-starved piece of human flotsam at the best of times. Thinking, he looked forlorn as well. Finally, he said: 'How much of this gold is to go out, Rem?'

'I ain't too sure. More than two shipments, I'd say.'

'Whose is it, or ain't I supposed to know?'

'You're not supposed to know, but it's Whiskey Joe's.'

Charlie whistled. Slightly off-key. He said: 'So the old coot finally pulled it off.'

'Bought a new house down the far end of Morrow. Looks right out over the valley. Got a pretty niece come in from Chicago to look out for him.'

'Ain't that something, now?' Charlie said in wonder.

'I have a feeling in my water,' McAllister said, 'that somebody's aiming to clean Joe out. I aim it shouldn't happen.'

'I aim it shouldn't happen just so long as I'm paid enough. I ain't a rich, horse-raising son-of-a-bitch money don't matter to. I'm just a poor and honest cowman –'

'This is Remington you're talking to, for God's sake,' said McAllister.

'Oh, yeah. I plumb forgot.' He rose. 'I have a notion to go visit with old Joe. Long time no see. Best look this niece over. Cowboys sure knock them city gals right off their pretty feet.'

'You do that,' said McAllister, who believed that beauty should be shared.

9

The following day, when the stage left Black Horse, it did so without paying passengers. This was by courtesy of Josiah Ramage, who compensated the stage company accordingly. Horry Wanlace, maintaining stoutly that if any member of this organisation was going to risk his neck it was going to be him, was up there on the box holding the ribbons. The messenger was McAllister. Inside the vehicle rode Charlie Stellino and Ham Stoppard. To say that they were armed to the teeth and loaded for bear would be to indulge in understatement.

The strong-box was not packed into the boot, but placed on the rear seat of the vehicle.

All they had to fear, McAllister said, was that once again the robbers would kill a horse from cover so that the stage was immobilised at the start of the operation. 'And', as he said, 'there ain't much anybody can do about that.'

'Except,' Charlie said, 'keep our eyes skinned and knock anybody over that looks like shooting in our direction.'

'That,' McAllister agreed, 'is a possibility, but if you kill some innocent standing beside the trail and minding his own business, you're on your own and it ain't any of the county's responsibility.'

'I have a feeling,' said Ham Stoppard, 'that we won't be stopped this time.'

'I have a feeling,' said McAllister, 'that you're right. Which is a state of affairs that suits me down to the ground.'

'Me too also,' said Charlie, 'I was not cut out to be a goddamn hero.'

Ham swallowed a few times and said: 'Ditto.' They looked at him in astonishment. For him, it was quite witty.

They climbed onto the stage and there was quite a crowd to see them off, notwithstanding the earliness of the hour, for they were starting some two hours before the scheduled time. J. Howard Lindholm danced on his toes, wished them luck and said that he could only wish he were going with them.

'Plenty of room inside, Mr Lindholm,' said Ham, and nobody knew if this was further wit or if he was being serious. Horry cracked his whip and cried out to his half-broken crew of unruly mustangs, and they once again raggedly hit their collars. They went out of town in some style, however, with Horry taking risks he would not have contemplated with paying passengers inside. They hit the bridge with about one inch to spare on the offiside and hit the slope beyond at a full gallop. Lindholm was heard to say: 'If those boys can't get through, nobody can.'

There was, of course, no hold-up. There was, though, a stop on the road, as chance would have it, almost on the exact spot where it had been halted by the road-agents before. This alarmed Ham Stoppard, who looked around under some emotion, searching for a target to shoot at.

McAllister jumped down from beside the driver and opened the stage door.

'All right,' he said, 'Ham, open up that strong-box.'

'W-what?' cried Ham, scandalised and incredulous. 'Not on your life, sheriff. I'll defend–'

Charlie said: 'Nobody ain't robbing you, Ham. You do have a key, don't you?'

'Sure I have a key, but you don't find me opening it.'

McAllister said: 'Ham, all we want to know is if we're really carrying gold. Me and Charlie are kind of funny that way. We hate to be killed for a few sacks of sand.'

'Sand?'

'Sand.'

Ham thought about that. They could see their reasoning seeping through to his understanding.

'I can see what you mean, fellers,' he said, 'but I don't know . . . Heck, I'm a servant of the bank and all that.'

McAllister said impatiently: 'We don't aim to stand around here all day, Ham, just in case there's bandits about. So go ahead and open it or we'll open it for you.'

'If you're that determined . . .' He searched in his pocket and produced a key. A moment later, the lid of the strong-box swung back and the tightly packed pokes were revealed to them.

'Open one up, Charlie,' McAllister said.

Charlie picked up a poke and untied the whang that held it closed. He took a pinch of dust between finger and thumb and placed it in McAllister's palm.

'That's gold, all right,' McAllister said. He put the dust back in the poke and Charlie tied it tight.

When the strong-box was locked again, Ham Stoppard said a little testily: 'I hope you're satisfied now.' They were, and the stage got on the move again.

'Maybe,' said McAllister to Horry, 'there's going to be a hold-up after all.'

'That's what I'm thinking,' said Horry.

But there was not. They were in Caspar by nightfall and handed their treasure over to the express company which would take it on to Chicago. They all had a pleasant evening in Caspar. They even got Ham Stoppard a little drunk, which they found mildly amusing. Charlie had a run-in with a local boy, an encounter which was followed pretty closely by another with the local law. McAllister was forced to dump him in a horse trough (full of water) before he could convince him that he himself was representing the law now and should behave accordingly. Horry Wanlace witnessed all this with expressions of the greatest delight, declaring that he had not had such a good time since he buried his old man.

They returned to Black Horse the following day in good spirits, liking the knowledge that they were unharmed by bandit bullets and had delivered their gold safely. I forget Ham Stoppard—he was not in good spirits, because he was somewhat hungover and looked it. Charlie told him that he was paying the penalty for leading a virtuous and sober life. If he was a boozer, he would not be suffering. Ham showed fight, but he cancelled the idea when he discovered that the top of his head flapped unaccountably when he clenched his fists.

McAllister returned to his town with the feeling that the next run to Caspar would be to guard a consignment of sand. He wondered if Ham would report to his boss that the strong-box had been opened and the contents inspected on the trail. He would probably never know. Certainly nothing was said about the matter.

There followed a week of nothing much happening. McAllister asked Charlie to ride the country to make a few discreet inquiries for him, but beyond that he bided his time. He worked a few days with his horses and paid court in a leisurely fashion on Miss Allison Disart. So did half the male population of the town below the age of eighty. Poor old Whiskey Joe's quiet life did not seem to be materialising. There were booted feet sounding on his back porch all hours of daylight. 'I never knew I was so damn popular,' he said. 'Sure is a comfort to have Ally here to entertain my guests.' Even Ham Stoppard came calling when he recovered from his hangover. He was the only one bold enough to bring flowers. Allison Disart blossomed under such treatment. Mark Tully, who should have known better, came calling, bringing with him a bottle of the finest rye for old Joe, which put him to the head of the queue, so far as Joe was concerned.

McAllister used some of Joe's money to have the

Pinkertons make some enquiries for him in Chicago. He was getting the feeling that the men who held up the stage and took the first consignment of gold were not here-today-and-gone-tomorrow kind of fellows. They were not a disease to be treated lightly, but a plague which had to be wiped out. If Black Horse country was to get a name for being an easy touch for thieves, a single simple hick sheriff was not going to be enough to hold the lid down on this neck of the woods. And he wanted to get back to his horses and forget about chasing badmen as if it was fun. A fellow could get himself hurt mortally doing that, and McAllister had heard enough bullets pass his left ear to last him the rest of his life.

He paid a visit to Black Ella who ran a few girls in pitiful shanties to the west of town. Ella was one of those souls who had forgotten how to eat, but survived somehow on a straight diet of rot-gut. She was not a whore with a heart of gold, but a madam who knew which side of her slice of bread bore the butter. She believed in collaborating with the law just so long as that did not interfere with business. There had been, she said, her little eyes snapping, no more than a few strangers among her clients in the last few weeks. Her custom was made up mostly of regulars and she wasn't going to name no names. That wasn't the way she ran her business. No gentleman wanted his wife to get to hear he was screwing outside the home. She described the few strangers. She gave good descriptions, because little eyes missed nothing. McAllister departed slightly wiser than when he had arrived, but not much.

He had confirmed that there were two strangers in town who might be able to help him in his enquiries. And there appeared to be no connection between the two of them. However, they had in common the habit of leaving town frequently and returning.

He decided to tread very carefully in his investigation of both of them. He could not, for example, go to Colonel English, who owned the Grand Union, and ply him with questions about Stevenson. The colonel was not what you might call a McAllister-lover. In any case, he suffered severely from a running off at the mouth.

As the day for the third run with a consignment from the bank for Caspar approached, McAllister kept a sharp eye on the Grand Union. The rooming house where the man Madders was staying could be seen from Whiskey Joe's new house and McAllister enlisted Joe to watch its front with a glass. So he was able to learn that Madders had left town the night before the stage run, and that Stevenson had ridden south soon after dawn. With something like confidence, McAllister told Charlie Stellino, as they prepared for the trail in the office: 'They'll stop the stage today, Charlie.'

Charlie looked a little sick, knowing that there would be lead flying and that he would have to put up a fight for his pay.

'Oh, God,' he said, 'here we go.'

'No,' said McAllister 'you don't go anywhere. You stay here. I want to know when Stevenson and Madders get back to town. And I want anything on them you can find out without asking questions. I don't want them suspicious.'

Charlie said: 'You really mean it?'

'I mean it.'

'Hallelujah!' Charlie cried with fervour.

McAllister walked over to the bank and found Lindholm and Ham Stoppard locking the strong-box. As he walked into the office, he heard old Horry Wanlace bringing the stage along the street.

McAllister said: 'Lindholm, do you reckon the stage'll be stopped today?'

Lindholm said: 'Now you ask me, sheriff, no I do not. I think the robbers were satisfied with what they got from the first robbery.'

McAllister said: 'Is that sand or gold in there?'

Lindholm looked shocked. 'Gold, of course.'

'All right, let's get it on board.'

When the stage was loaded and ready to move, Lindholm said to Ham: 'Now, Ham, no drinking this time, mind.'

'No, Mr Lindholm.' Ham climbed into the stage. There were two or three local men inside already. McAllister swung himself up beside Horry and the whip cracked.

Nothing happened on the first part of the journey, but, as the stage slowed to a walk to climb the rise where the first hold-up had taken place, McAllister told Horry that he could see riders in the timber above them.

'Horry,' he said, 'when you get near the top and should be at your slowest, can you lay on the whip and put the horses at a dead run?'

'Sure. The horses ain't going to like it, but I don't suppose they get a lot of fun out of pulling a stage, anyway.'

When the horses had reduced their pace to their slowest walk, all of them straining forward in their collars, McAllister lifted his Henry and started firing into the trees and rocks on either side of the trail. At the same moment, Horry gave a shrill cry and laid on the whip. For a second, it seemed that his efforts would have no effect, but suddenly the stage lurched forward and bounded over the crest of the hill. It was halfway down by the time the riders were down out of timber and racing their mounts along the road. McAllister fired back at them, and they did not hold their pursuit for more than a half-minute before they pulled off the road and disappeared. By this time, the half-broken team had bolted, and they ran for a mile before Horry could pull them down to a steady trot.

'By God,' said Horry,' that there was a piece of smart action if ever I saw it.' Inside the stage, the local men were cheering. Ham Stoppard put head and shoulders out of a window to yell up at McAllister: 'That sure showed 'em, sheriff.'

'Yes,' McAllister bawled back, 'and all for a box of goddam sand.'

'Beg pardon,' said Ham.

'By golly,' said one of the local men to the other, 'we'll have something to tell the folks about when we get back.'

'Sure will,' replied the other.

Ham Stoppard was a little put out when they halted at the express office in Caspar and McAllister told him he could pour the contents of the strong-box out on the street. There were a few rather warm words between them when

McAllister refused to help Ham tote the box into the express office.

'I ain't sweating over a heap of sand,' McAllister declared.

'That's gold,' said Ham. 'I swear it's gold.'

'I swear it's sand. How about a hundred-dollar bet on it?'

Ham turned quite pale even at the thought of betting a hundred dollars on anything, even a certainty. It took him some time to be persuaded to open the box. When he saw that the contents were sand, he gave a fine performance of a man totally surprised. McAllister almost believed in him.

'Next time,' McAllister threatened, 'I see the box before it's packed. This is the last time I risk my hide for a heap of sand.'

That night Ham hung on a good one and McAllister had to dump him into the selfsame horse trough. McAllister was beginning to worry about the boy. For one reason or another, or maybe one reason and another, he was starting to go to pieces.

Ham rode back to Black Horse the following day on top of the stage, because he could not bear to be confined. Even with the windows wide to the world he found the vehicle airless. He swore off strong drink for the rest of his life.

'You're wasting your time,' McAllister snarled. He was never good in the early hours of morning. 'You should swear off being in cahoots with a bank owner to dupe poor sheriffs and sparking lovely dark-haired girls.' Ham had the grace to blush scarlet. Whether it was at the mention of the banker or the girl, McAllister would never know.

10

When McAllister reported the whole business to Lindholm, the banker was furious. Well, let us say that he was furious at first. He burst out about sacred trust and a lot more of that kind of thing. He said that he would fire Ham and that he would have McAllister's badge. Ham said if he felt like that, he would happily resign. In truth, he was still too hungover to care much what happened to him and seemed to be existing in a haze of unreality. McAllister took off his badge and tossed it on to the banker's desk. At this point, Lindholm seemed to switch his mood right around. Suddenly, he was greatly appreciative of the great risk both of them were taking. All this gold had been a great worry to him. They must bear with him. He would find some way of rewarding them. He shook them both by the hand. There would be one more shipment of this lot of gold, and then they would rethink the whole situation.

McAllister said: 'You'll have to do a whole lot of thinking, Lindholm. Now that the other prospectors are here.'

That startled the banker. 'What prospectors?'

'They are starting to come into the country,' McAllister told him. 'The word always gets out, no matter how careful you are. You know how it is.'

The banker nodded and nodded. Indeed he did. He must protect Joe's interests. That was his sworn duty, as it was the duty of every banker to protect his clients. If Joe would reveal where his gold lay so that a proper arrangement could be made . . . Couldn't McAllister talk to him, persuade him. Joe was an old man and he needed looking after.

'I've tried,' McAllister said. 'Joe's a stubborn old man.'

'Try again,' said Lindholm. 'Don't give up trying. I have a feeling harm will come to the old fellow if we don't do something. According to him, the gold we have shipped is nothing compared with what is still in the ground.' He fixed his eyes on McAllister. 'I have a feeling that he has not staked his claim, you know. He must stake his claim. Then we'll know.'

'I'll have another try,' said McAllister.

As he walked away from the bank, he thought about that. All he could think of was that Joe must be watched, somehow or other, around the clock.

When he walked into the office, he found Charlie Stellino there. He had already heard about the failed attack on the stage.

After expressing his pleasure at not having been present, Charlie said: 'You sure they was only fooling, Rem?'

'We surprised them all right when Horry whipped up his team,' McAllister said, 'but we did not surprise them all that much. They know their business too well for that, Charlie. No, they had to show they were after the gold, because they couldn't afford to let us know they knew there was only sand in the strong-box. There's somebody on the inside who knows as much or more than us.'

'So who's on the inside?'

'That we know of – old Joe himself, Lindholm and Ham Stoppard.'

'That's it. There ain't nobody else.'

'There's the other clerk in the bank, and there's the girl.'

'How about the expressman in Caspar?'

'He don't know the gold's coming.'

'Well,' said Charlie, 'we can rule out Ham and the girl.'

'We don't rule anybody out,' said McAllister.

'Hell,' said Charlie, 'don't we?'

They took one small drink together, just to oil the weariness of the day from their throats. They sat around the office while McAllister cleaned and oiled his weapons, which had suffered from the dust of the road. They talked. Charlie was a man who was smarter than he talked. Which was just as well.

He said: 'Rem, one of us has got to track them fellers back from the next hold-up. There ain't no other way of pulling anything off against them.'

'We're thinking the same,' said McAllister. 'Which means, most likely, they're thinking the same thing.'

'You agree they're going to hit the last consignment of gold to go out?'

'Yes,' said McAllister, 'I agree.'

'So this is our last chance.'

'Certainly for some time.'

Charlie said: 'I thought about this a lot. You'll have to ride inside with a good horse tied on behind.'

'I had the same idea. Then I remembered how they shot that leader at their first hist. If I tie a horse behind, likely they'll know what it's for and they'll take it or shoot it.'

'You could be right. So you have to trail the stage.'

'How can you trail the stage in the open without being spotted?'

'So what the hell do we do? We have no idea where they'll hit us this next time.'

'That's right.' McAllister assembled his revolver in silence. He loaded it and frowned. 'There's only one way to do it. I'll have to be hidden somewhere along the trail, at the Caspar end. I wait till the stage reaches me and tells me where it was stopped. Then I come back and start tracking. It's a hell of a gamble, but can you think of any other way?'

'No, I can't,' said Charlie. 'Maybe it wouldn't be a bad idea to have somebody this end of the road on the off-chance they might see the hold-up. That way we would have the chance of at least two riders in the chase.'

McAllister eyed him speculatively. 'Maybe,' he said. 'Yes, that makes sense. Me the far end of the road and you somewhere halfway, say the spot where they stopped the stage before.'

'I'll go along with that,' Charlie said. There was no doubt or anxiety in his face now. He could see the action. Charlie was always at his best when the action looked concrete.

'So,' said McAllister. 'That's settled. Now, how about our friends. When did they get back into town?'

'Madders got in from the south around seven in the evening. Stevenson came in after dark, say, ten. Their horses had been ridden some. Madders' horse had a bullet burn along its nearside flank. He didn't offer any explanation for it. Just showed surprise when it was pointed out to him.'

McAllister looked vexed. 'My shooting wasn't ever that bad,' he said.

'You were on a moving stage.'

'Must have been from one of his friends' bullets.

Charlie looked sceptical. McAllister gave him another drink and sent him out to watch Joe Ramage's house.

Lige Copley rode into town to report on the ranch and receive orders. He and McAllister talked horses for an hour or more and McAllister bought him a meal at the Chinese restaurant. Lige put more food away into his beanstalk frame than a man four times his size would have been ashamed to be seen consuming in public. McAllister did not know whether to feel proud or embarrassed. Wu Song, who owned the restaurant, said: 'Jeez Clist, I never seen nobody eat nothing like it.'

Lige rode off into the sunset, and McAllister returned to the office at the same time Charlie arrived. He said: 'That feller Stevenson just called on Joe. They're drinking the old man's best liquor. That Allison gal is a-hovering around them till it sickens you to see it.'

'You're jealous.'

'That's right.'

McAllister buckled on his gun. Charlie said: 'Where you going?'

McAllister told him: 'Miss Allison should be sparked by local men only. I'm going to prise her loose from the interloper.'

Charlie said earnestly: 'You're a man who knows his duty.'

'Ain't I?' said McAllister. 'Take a badge over to Mark Tully and tell him to stuff it in his pocket. I have a feeling we're going to need old Mark around here before we're through.'

'I know where Mark'll tell you to stuff that badge.'

McAllister smiled sadly and went out.

He did not hurry himself down to Joe's house, because he was pretty sure that Stevenson would be in no hurry to leave, and not only because of the lovely girl, either. Because of the lovely gold.

His knock on the street door was answered by the girl, as he had hoped.

'Good evening, sheriff,' she said.

He went to enter, but found her in his path. 'I'm here to talk to Joe,' he said.

'Uncle Joe is engaged at this moment,' she said.

McAllister took off his hat politely and said: 'Folks disengage when the sheriff calls officially.'

She hesitated. 'I'll tell him you're here,' and turned away from the door.

He followed close behind her and said: 'No call, ma'am.' She was a little mad, but there was not much she could do about it. McAllister followed her right through the house to the back porch.

Old Joe cried out: 'Why, Rem, this sure is a pleasure. Have a drink?'

'Miss Allison told me you were engaged. Joe. Sorry –'

'Engaged? Hell, I ain't engaged. Just jawing with a new friend here. Stevenson, meet McAllister. He's the law in the parts, such as it is. Ha! Ha!'

'Ha! ha! ha!' said Stevenson. He rose to greet McAllister, who found his hand grip dry and firm.

Joe said: 'We was having a mighty interesting talk, Rem. Mighty interesting. Stevenson is a mining man. Knows all there is to know about gold and stuff.'

McAllister was genial. He beamed on host and fellow guest, and extended his great smile warmly to the girl.

'I'd bet a thousand dollars,' he said, 'I know what you're talking about, Joe.'

'That's a lot of money,' said Joe.

'Not for you.'

'Ha! ha! ha!' said Joe.

'Ha! ha! ha!' said Stevenson. Even the girl smiled. Joe beamed a million dollars' worth of happiness.

'What?' said Joe.

'Mr Stevenson was telling you that for your own sake you should disclose the whereabouts of your mine. You should get organised properly and et cetera.'

Joe cried: 'That's it. That's what we was talking about.'

'Uncanny,' said the stranger.

'I'll bet old Lindholm is trying to sell you the same idea,' said McAllister.

'That about the size of it,' said Joe.

McAllister found a seat and accepted the drink the girl offered him. He drank, and found the rye excellent. He said: 'You're keeping a good cellar, Joe.'

'Yeah,' said Joe. 'A man in my position . . . '

'You hear the road agents made another try at the stage, Joe?'

'Is that a fact?'

'Sure is. But we pulled a fast one on them.'

Stevenson enquired: 'What happened exactly, sheriff?'

'Why,' said McAllister, 'we were approaching the spot where the road agents stopped the stage before. It's just the right place for a hyste. The road is so steep that the team is at a slow walk. I told old Horry to whip up the team at the last moment because I'd spotted riders among the trees. We went over the brow of the hill without the wheels touching. They came after us, firing off their pieces, but they were too late. We got clean away into Caspar with the gold intact.'

'That sure is great news,' said Joe.

'But it backs up my claim, Mr Ramage,' said Stevenson, 'that while there's gold, there's danger for you. Sheriff, I'm trying to talk Mr Ramage into considering a business partnership. I'm an engineer, and I could get the gold out of those hills in no time at all. It'd squeeze our work-time down and lessen the danger-time. You see that, don't you? Most likely a year or less would see us through. By engineering the process properly we could extract a far higher percentage of gold, making anything you paid me amply financed over and over by the greater gain.'

McAllister said: 'There's a lot in what he says, Joe. I'd think on it.'

Joe looked a little sulky. 'All right,' he said, 'I'll think on it.'

'If I could have a look at your claim, Mr. Ramage,' said Stevenson, 'that would given me a chance to assess its potential.'

Old Joe looked a little wild. He cried: 'You'd assess your potential too, I dare say.'

Stevenson protested. 'All I look for is a legitimate return for my time and trouble, Mr Ramage. The extra gold modern methods would produce would more than compensate me.'

Joe said: 'I ain't revealing the whereabouts of my claim, and that's final.'

'Take me to it blindfold,' said Stevenson. 'Nobody's trying to rob you.'

'Like hell they ain't,' Joe yelled, going falsetto. 'They took a whole load of gold, didn't they? What do you call that?'

McAllister said: 'I think we've seen the last hold-up, Joe. They learned their lesson yesterday. Our guard on the stage is too much for 'em.'

Stevenson said: 'Sure looks like it.'

He made his apologies and departed shortly after. The girl went with him to the street door.

Joe looked at McAllister balefully. 'They're all the same. They come whining and cringing around me now I have the gold. Nobody passed the time of day civilly with me before I had it.'

'Joe,' McAllister said, 'I'll give it to you blunt and fast while we don't have anybody listening.'

Joe went still, leaning forward and listening. 'Shoot.'

'Either they'll squeeze the truth out of you here, Joe, or they'll follow you to the mine. Either way, you're dead.'

McAllister watched a number of emotions reflected on the old man's face. Fear and alarm, scorn, rage, wariness.

'You're just trying to make me tell you,' he said. 'I wouldn't even tell the girl.'

McAllister said: 'Did Allison ask you where the gold is?'

Only wariness showed on the old face now. 'You ain't suspecting her, for crissakes?'

'When it comes to gold, Joe, I suspect everybody. I'm asking one thing. If they threaten you and you reckon they mean it, you tell 'em, Joe. I have a feeling these men'll stop at nothing. Just tell 'em and leave the rest to me. My word on it, they won't get your gold.'

The old man gave that some thought. He was impressed, that much was plain. The girl came back and stood looking slightly puzzled from one to the other of them.

Joe said: 'I'll study on it, boy.' McAllister said he had to be going. When they reached the street door and the girl opened it, he looked down at her and gazed into those clear, honest blue eyes. To see such transparent truth gave him a strange feeling. He said: 'Stay close, Miss Allison. I think Joe may be in real danger. You suspect anything, you let me know.'

She said: 'I'll do that, sheriff. It's a real comfort to know you're around.'

McAllister thought that was nicely put. He gave her his best smile and headed for the white picket gate.

Back at his office, he got out the cot so that Charlie and he could take turns getting a sleep. Charlie thought this watching Joe's house all night was taking security too damn far, but McAllister did not relent. It occurred to him, during the long watch of the night, his Navaho poncho around his shoulders against the cold, that a good time for the bandits to make a move against Joe would be while he, McAllister, was out of town with the gold. Mentally, he shrugged his shoulders. Not even he could be in two places at once. During the night it came on to rain and the water got inside his collar and ran down his back. There was nothing he disliked more, and he began to wonder if Charlie was not right and this business was getting ridiculous. Just the same, his old Indian foreboding was starting to haunt him.

He was not in too good a mood when he went into the Chinese restaurant for breakfast. Charlie joined him and said: 'Just looking at you tells me you don't think this foolery a good idea no longer.'

'We go on doing it just the same,' McAllister said stubbornly.

Charlie said: 'They seem to know everything we do, so

why don't they know about us watching Joe's place?'

'Because we didn't tell anybody,' said McAllister. 'Or did one of us?' His eye on Charlie was terrible.

Charlie shivered a little and said: 'This one didn't. I don't know about that one.'

11

All they gained from the watch was loss of sleep and an increase in irritability. McAllister called in at the bank and confirmed with Lindholm that he thought it was safe to withdraw extra guards from the stage when the gold was shipped out. The last of it, thank God, said McAllister.

'You can say that again,' said the banker. 'I've had enough of the worry. Let somebody else take over. I and my man Stoppard are quite worn down with it all. No, no further need for extra guards, sheriff.'

'In that case,' said McAllister, 'I'll go back to horse-ranching for a few days. My business is all to hell.'

'You do that, McAllister, with the clearest of consciences. You have done more than your duty and the bank is grateful to you. I, personally, am grateful to you. Joe sings your praises every time I talk with him.'

McAllister gave a good impression of a man glowing and said: 'That's really nice to hear, Lindholm. I sure do appreciate that.'

He rode back to his place and ate a second breakfast. He had been deprived of Bella Copley's cooking long enough.

'Bella,' he said, 'those two men of yours sure don't appreciate you. How about moving in with me?'

She laughed and said: 'Landsakes, Miz McAllister, we is scandal enough already.'

Mose glowered and said: 'Some fellers don't naturally know when they is best off.'

When McAllister was through eating, he jerked his head at Mose as a signal he wanted a quiet word with him out of Bella's hearing. Mose joined him in the barn. So far, the blacksmith did not know more than he had heard in town about the problem of Joe's gold. Now McAllister told him, and Mose did not like what he heard.

'The way you tell it,' he said, 'tells me you think this is going to turn into an ugly business, boss.'

'That's the way she looks. I hate to pull you in on this, Mose, but could you watch Joe's place tomorrow night. Maybe Charlie or me can't make it back in time.'

'Sure. But how about Bella? She'll raise hell.'

'She always raises hell.'

'That's a fact.'

McAllister enjoyed a good night's sleep, rose a couple of hours before dawn and saddled Oscar, his powerful gelding. He caught up his mare, Sally, and put her on a hackamore and a hair rope as a lead line. Lige appeared from out of the dark, like a sombre thin ghost.

'Boss, I can see by the looks of you, you ain't up to no good.'

McAllister smiled. 'Just lawing a piece, Lige.'

'You want me along.'

'Mose'll be out for me. You stay here and watch the store.'

'Hell, I ain't never nothing but horse-holder and store-keeper. Don't I never get into the action?'

'Before we're through, Lige,' McAllister told him earnestly, 'there'll be more than enough action to go around. Believe me.'

Lige watched him solemnly and said: 'I believe you.'

McAllister mounted Oscar and rode out. When he had crossed Howard Creek, he rode straight across the valley for the foothills and was well on his way by daylight. He was in position above the place where the first hold-up had taken place. From there, a short while after, he saw a lone horseman coming from town and recognised him as Charlie. Satisfied, he now rode on, travelling at a good speed, knowing now that he did not have a great deal of time to spare.

12

When Charlie rode into high timber at the station he was to take up, he saw the hoofprints left by McAllister's horses in the still damp ground. It had not rained since the night before last, but the rain then had been heavy and there was still an amount of moisture in the ground under the trees. Charlie hoped there would be a better than usual chance of following tracks. He dismounted and led his horse well back into the trees, not wanting the animal to betray his presence.

When he had returned to his position above the road, he was startled to see two horsemen below him, between him and the road. It was alarming for him to know they could arrive there without his either seeing or hearing them. He looked around uneasily. He checked the position of the pale sun and saw that more than an hour would pass before the stage was due. He peered into the trees, shrub and boulders on the far side of the road. His sharp eyes at once picked out the dark shape of a hat. Then the sun hit the barrel of a carbine. He knew that he was lucky to have arrived so early. He could so easily have ridden right into the muzzles of those guns down there.

The bandits seemed to settle down then. He saw the blue smoke of their cigarettes. Once or twice, the soft murmur of voices reached him. It was no more than a few minutes, however, before he grew alarmed, for one of the men on his side of the road rose abruptly to his feet and started up the steep slope towards Charlie. He could see from the man's manner that he was looking for somebody or something. His companion was on his feet, scanning the slope.

Charlie hastily started to make his way backwards, then, once he was in deep shelter, turned and hurried on, going over the brow of the hill and down towards his horse.

At first, when he could not see his horse, he looked around, thinking that he was mistaken in the spot. Then he thought maybe the animal had gotten free and strayed off.

There came a shrill whistle from the top of the hill and an answering one from below him and he thought: *I'm caught plumb in between the two of them. They made a damn fool out of me.*

That scared him. But scared or not, Charlie Stellino was not a man to be beaten. He got in among the thickets and started to beat his way west as quietly as he could. Pretty soon, he ran out of thicket and was forced into the open. He wondered if the men would risk shooting. The shots might be heard. But maybe they were sure that there was nobody near.

He knew the answer to that one in the next second.

He heard a shot to his right. It passed so close to him that he jumped a foot. It ripped its way through the leaves and, almost at once, there came a shot from another direction. He was in a crossfire. He was, in fact, as good as dead. That was not enough, however, to make him give up the fight. He jacked a round into the breech of his Spencer and fired as he saw a branch move. At once there was return fire from both directions. Something smashed into his side and knocked him from his feet.

There was something so brutal, final and disastrous about being hit that he almost gave up the ghost. What the hell, he asked himself, was there anything here worth dying for? Would McAllister ask the ultimate sacrifice of him?

No time for answers. A man crashed through the undergrowth and, lying on his back, Charlie fired and levered, fired and levered. There was a slight movement off to his left and he turned his gun muzzle in that direction, still firing.

He heard a man yell and swear.

Undergrowth seemed to be crashing all around him. He doubted if he could make it to his feet, but he had under-estimated the strength of fear. He was up and going at a staggering run. He had not gone a dozen uncertain paces when he ran headlong into the bulk of an object in his path, an object that seemed to stagger back from his charge. He nearly fell over himself and then saw, to his utter astonishment, that he had run into his own horse tied to a tree.

Laughing like a crazy man, he tore the line free of the tree and heaved himself into the saddle. The horse must have understood his predicament, for, no sooner had his backside hit leather than the animal gathered its legs under it and jumped away. Charlie thought he heard the faint sound of shots behind him, but he could not be sure. He did not much care. When he looked back, nobody followed. He reined his horse around to the road, hit it within minutes and let the horse run east. With luck he would reach McAllister before he bled to death.

13

McAllister was not too pleased to see Charlie, nor was he satisfied that he had carried out his duties as a duly-sworn deputy.

'Duly-sworn deputy?' Charlie said in disgust as he lay bleeding on the ground. 'When the hell was I ever duly-sworn? All you ever did was shove a goddam badge in my face.'

'And your wages,' McAllister snarled. 'Don't forget your wages, you ungrateful son-of-a-bitch. You come running for help just because you got your fool self nicked in the side. I should of brought young Lige along; he'd have done the job better.'

Charlie said: 'Do you fix me up or do I bleed to death? Don't forget, if I die, the county pays for the funeral.'

McAllister's mood changed and he laughed. 'You're sure unlucky, Charlie,' he said. 'You ain't going to die, boy. It'll cost you your shirt. Get it off. And hurry, we don't have all the time in the world.' To show that he bore Charlie no ill-feeling, he offered him a pull from his bottle. It was not a large bottle and Charlie finished it, a fact which tried McAllister's goodwill to the utmost. However, he tied Charlie's wound up well enough and declared that if his evil living had not corrupted his body too much, there was a chance that he would live. 'We'll put you on the stage and the doctor in Caspar can sew you up good as new.'

'Aw, hell,' said Charlie, 'I can sit a horse, Rem. I can track down one of the bandits.'

'I'd hate to put your delicate frame to the test,' said McAllister coldly.

Charlie said something which was both insulting and obscene. The sheriff ignored him. Not long after, the stage came along with an irate and murderous Horry Wanlace on the other end of the ribbons. The bandits had shot another horse, he told them. They had carried out the whole operation as smooth as silk. Wally Hunt had apparently simulated fear very well and not fired a shot. The robbers had taken the strong-box and seen the stage on its way.

'This,' said Horry, 'is the last time I play this game, Rem, and that's final. Christ, I'm getting through horses so damn fast...'

'This is the very last time, Horry,' McAllister promised.

They packed Charlie into the stage, and the last McAllister heard of him, he was telling the passengers that he had held off a dozen wild outlaws with his gun.

McAllister mounted Oscar and, leading the mare, he set off back down the road. He did not hurry, because he knew that he might be facing several days of riding and he wanted his horses fresh. He was at the hold-up spot about one hour later. Dismounting and tying his horses at the side of the road, he took a leisurely look around at the tracks left on either side of the road. He wanted to read them well and he wanted to be sure of his facts before he decided to follow a set. Pretty soon he was confident that he would have plain sign to follow. As before, there had been four men in the hold-up and one spare horse. This horse had been employed to carry away the strong-box. Two riders had gone with the box this time. They had taken the direction which McAllister had followed previously. It was simple reasoning to assume that they would go by way of the watersmeet where he had lost the tracks before. He would have liked to regain the gold this trip, but it was no good trying to tackle the impossible. One set of tracks went off almost parallel to the Caspar road. The other looked as if it was heading back into Black Horse Valley. This was the one he decided to follow.

That was his first mistake, maybe.

He walked back to his horse, thrust a foot into the stirrup iron and started to heave himself into the saddle. A voice behind him said: 'Hold it.'

He did just that. There was no doubt in his mind that a gun was pointed at his spine.

The voice said: 'Put one foot on the ground and stay right there.'

He obeyed, knowing that, in that position, he was pretty helpless. He heard the man take a few paces towards him, and the next moment the weight of his old Remington went from his side.

'My, my,' he said, 'I thought I was too old to be suckered. How a man fools himself.'

The man said: 'Cut out the talk. I'm the one who talks.'

'You're spooked,' McAllister said. 'What the hell do you have to be spooked about? You're holding the gun.'

'Cut it out,' said the man. His voice rose a little in excitement. McAllister heard his sharp intake of breath and knew that a gun-barrel was about to land on his head. He tightened his grip on the cantle and horn of the saddle and heaved his weight up one inch. At the same time, he kicked back as hard as he could with the heel of his right boot.

By the jarring sensation it gave him, he reckoned he

caught the man on the breastbone. The man gave a deep grunt and his gun went off.

Now, there is nothing like fear either to concentrate a man's thoughts and faculties or completely paralyse them. In this case, happily for McAllister, his senses were acutely sharpened by the fact that there was a gun in the hand of the other man, even though that man was going over backwards as McAllister got his foot out of the stirrup-iron and whirled. His sharp eye took the man in, seeing a heavily-made, square man who looked as solid as rock. Slightly below average height, but long in the arm. As he came in McAllister's sight he was out of control, falling back onto his shoulders, dropping his own gun from his right hand, but retaining his grip on McAllister's with his left. His fingers were around the chamber, not the butt. McAllister kicked savagely at the butt and saw the weapon spin away. He now stamped down hard onto the fellow's belly.

Any other man would have been finished by the assault. As it was, though the air went noisily out of him, he grasped at McAllister's booted foot with both hands and tore him from his feet.

McAllister had been thrown a good many times during the passage of a violent life, but he could never remember when his own large body had been treated as such light-weight stuff. He hit the ground badly, with one arm caught under him. He heard the man say in fury through his clenched teeth: 'I'm going to kill you, you bastard.' The fellow then climbed slowly and relentlessly to his feet, retaining his grip on McAllister's ankle.

McAllister drove with his free foot at the man's hands, cracking his hard boot-heel down on his knuckles. But he might have been punishing stone. The man then did something which McAllister thought could never happen to him. He was wrenched off the ground and found himself being whirled around in that powerful grip, circling with his face near the ground and feeling utterly helpless. He was not released until the nearest tree came up from nowhere to meet his chest. Then the man released him.

McAllister lay on the ground for a moment, feeling as if

his chest had been crushed in and that every bone in his body loosed from its natural fastening. But his old alarm system was sounding. He looked up to see the man in mid-air, both boots descending.

Again, fear was his spur. He moved, and he moved fast, but managing no more than a half-roll before the fellow landed. No more was required. The man cracked down onto the ground and fell against the tree which had just so severely punished McAllister.

The big man slewed himself around on the ground, driving himself into the other man's legs and knocking them from under him. The man hit the tree with his face and fell to the ground. He had suffered, but not enough to deter him. He rose to his feet at the same speed attained by McAllister. For a moment, they stood panting, two apparent equals, both with blood-splattered faces and punished bodies.

The man took a deep breath and managed: 'Kill you.'

McAllister saved his breath. He hit the man twice. Both blows were delivered with his left. One landed on his mouth and the other on his nose. The last made a surprising amount of noise.

The man's voice sounded a little mushy when he said: 'That won't do you no good. I'm still going to kill you.'

He aimed a kick for McAllister's crotch. McAllister batted the foot aside and hit the man on his neck. The blow staggered him backwards.

McAllister said: 'That's not two-twenty pounds of muscle and bone you have there. You're full of crap.'

The man charged and McAllister thought: *If he gets those arms around me, I'm finished.*

His opponent could move fast enough for a man half his weight. Those arms did get around McAllister, and at once his ribs began to crumble. McAllister rammed his feet against the man's insteps and heaved himself backwards, turning as best he could as he did so. They landed on their sides, and the man retained his grip. McAllister thought he heard his ribs crack. He heard the man whisper: 'Kill you, you bastard.' McAllister tried to butt the man's face, but his height was against him and all he could do was bang his chin on top of the fellow's head. For his pains, he received that hard skull under his jaw. His senses started to waver. His sight did not seem so good either. The pressure on his ribs increased. The man's breathing was shallow and fierce.

With a heave which seemed to drain the last strength from his body, McAllister rolled and got himself on top. Now he managed to get one elbow under the fellow's throat and against his chin, and the contest turned into a test of strength against strength. Right at the start, McAllister knew he could not win. This man would crack all his ribs and then stomp him into the ground at his leisure.

Bright lights darted wildly before McAllister's eyes. He wrenched and heaved in a savagely frantic attempt to get free.

'Kill you,' whispered the man.

McAllister was pretty sure now that the threat would be carried out in something like a half-minute.

He tried to increase his pressure on the other's throat. He looked down and saw to his surprise that the man's eyes were starting from his head. He tore his other arm free and gripped the man's ears with both hands. The fellow tried to whisper his threat of death, but could not make it. McAllister started to lift his head and ram it down onto the ground. Luck had found him a tree root. The man gave a long low moan and his grip on McAllister started to slacken.

McAllister rolled violently to the right and found himself free, and he told himself: no more of this damn nonsense of man-to-man. He wanted a gun. He went after the butt of the Remington in a low long dive. And he knew from the sounds that the man had a similar idea. The road agent must have reached a gun first. Even as McAllister hit dirt and rolled, he heard the roar of the heavy gun. Something tore up the dirt by him and he fired blindly and cocked again for a second shot. He could dimly see the man up on one knee. He triggered a shot. The man grunted and put his other hand to the gun to heave back on the hammer, which seemed to be resisting him. McAllister fired again.

This time, the fellow went backwards, rolling over down the slight slope and coming up against the bole of the tree.

McAllister stayed very still, watching him kick a little. Then he sat up and found that he did not have the strength to move further. He started to shake.

14

When he had found the dead man's horse, which had been tied at a distance of about a quarter-mile from the hold-up point, McAllister picked up the tracks of the man going into the valley and followed them. He did not waste any time, for now he was conscious of a sense of urgency. The chance that the shots had been heard was too great for his comfort. Not because of personal danger. He was troubled that his recovery of the gold and his arrest of the culprits might be prevented.

He was in a strange and uneasy frame of mind, for the encounter with the man who now lay dead among the trees had shaken him. He had come as near as he had ever been to being killed by another man's bare hands. And the need for a killing had come upon him too much unawares. Now, he told himself, a man had died. This was the point a sane lawman never wanted to reach. Once the guns were out, a milestone had been passed. Gangs of lawless men reacted always in the same way to such a killing. Their own reluctance to kill would now be removed. He could only hope that it would be some time before the men discovered their loss. He wondered also if the dead man had kin or a close friend among the remainder of the bunch. The last thing McAllister wanted was to be opposed by a man dedicated to his demise.

Feeling mentally and physically battered, he headed down into the valley, leading his two horses after him. The captured animal was a fine-drawn bay with a delicate manner and an alert eye. Altogether a good and amiable animal. It was a gelding that followed along nicely with the mare, Sally.

The damp nature of the ground made the first part of the tracking job a cinch. Any fool could have done it. But once McAllister was down out of the foothills into the valley itself, he found that the rider had turned his mount sharply across the valley on the shortest route either to Howard Creek or to the town road beyond. The man might lose his tracks in the creek or, if the traffic was heavy enough, in the recent tracks on the road itself. By noon, the fellow could be safe in town.

Maybe not so safe. The man would be a stranger, and strangers were always noticed in small towns.

At the same time, McAllister was acutely aware that the man was not necessarily a stranger. He hoped fervently that he was not a local man. Local men had kin and friends and an arrest, like a wounding or killing, could lead to trouble which could dribble on through generations. But he would worry about that kind of thing when he came to it.

It was past noon when he halted on the bank of the creek and saw where the man's horse had entered the water. It had done so at an exact right-angle to the bank, giving him not the slightest idea which direction the man may have taken. He took his horses across with the water coming up to his stirrup-irons. The flow was fairly strong and the horses were inclined to drift with it. He took them up the far bank, dismounted and tied them to a willow there. Now, he ranged on foot up and down the bank searching both sides for any sign of the man landing and found none. He knew that the man could have ridden the creek all the way north to the end of the valley, gone into the Breaks and headed for town through the western hills. Just the same, he reckoned he should take a gamble and make a few short-cuts himself. Speed was important now. He found that he was starting to get a little rattled and he did not like that one little bit. None of this business was working out as he had planned. He reckoned he had over-estimated himself. Maybe it would do him good to eat a little humble pie.

He hurried back to his horses and sent them at a run along the road for home.

Lige was in the yard, all gangling length and wide eyes. He registered the strange horse and McAllister's battered appearance.

McAllister swung out of the saddle and said: 'Lige, you listen good and answer me real smart, hear?' The boy nodded. 'Any riders been past here in the last couple of hours, on the road, off the road, even along the creek bed?'

Lige thought. He wanted to ask questions. What had happened? Why was McAllister's face bloody? Who owned the strange horse? But he dared not. He said: 'Ranch buckboard come along the road from the north soon after first light. There was a man rid along the ridge through the trees maybe an hour back. Going toward town. Mr Mittlehouse's foreman come over the crick a while back. Ain't seen hide nor hair of nobody else.'

'Where's your pa?'

'He went off for town yesterday. Told ma he was doing a chore for you, boss. He ain't come home and ma is a-worrying some.'

McAllister passed the horses' lines to him and said: 'Saddle the mare and throw the other two into the starve-out. Feed 'em both.'

Lige said: 'Mr Tully sent word. If you come home you was to get yourself into town like the heel flies was after you.'

'All right,' said McAllister. 'See to the horses. I'll go see your ma.'

But Bella Copley was on her way and she was running, which was not a thing she did often, for she was a woman of some dignity. Now her pretty face was shining with sweat and her eyes were worried.

'Miz McAllister,' she said before she reached him, 'what happen to my man?'

'I don't know, Bella.'

She stopped and stared at his face. 'You been hurt.'

'Some.'

'Is Mose in trouble?'

'I thought he'd be safe enough,' McAllister said and felt

guilty as hell. He did not have the right to drag the Copleys into this. 'I don't know now. Not after what happened.'

'Is Mose in town?'

'Should be.'

'I want to go to him.'

McAllister hesitated. Then he said: 'Sure. Lige, leave these horses to me. Catch up the buckboard team and hitch 'em. Pronto.'

Lige knew when speed was wanted. And he could move. He grabbed a rope and went over the corral fence in a flash. McAllister unsaddled Oscar and put his rig on the mare. He wheeled out the buckboard and in no time at all he and Lige had backed the team into it and hitched them. He handed Bella onto the buckboard and tied the mare on behind. Then he jumped up beside Bella and lifted the lines.

'Lige,' he said, 'you stay close now.' Then he cracked the whip around the ears of the two horses and they hit their traces together. He went out of the yard like a bat out of hell and Bella clung onto him.

As they swung out onto the road and the horses stretched out for town, McAllister said: 'Bella, you start giving me hell and you'll be wasting your breath. I'm giving it myself already.'

'So you should, Miz McAllister,' said Bella.

Mark Tully was standing on the sidewalk outside the saloon when McAllister drew rein. Mark was frowning, and he had one of those frowns which seemed to darken the whole world around him. He helped Bella down from the buckboard as McAllister tied the lines and put the whip away.

Mark told Bella: 'He's in my back room, Bella. He's going to be all right. The doc's seen to him.' She hurried inside.

McAllister walked around the buckboard and said: 'What happened?'

Mark said: 'How the hell should I know what happened? Some kid found Mose in deep timber beyond Joe Ramage's house. Somebody had beaten him, but good. I would reckon they'd left him for dead. They just didn't have a notion how tough old Mose is. But he sure don't look pretty.'

'And Joe?'

'Joe? Why, as far as I know he's still on his back porch counting his millions.'

'Any strangers ridden into town this morning?'

'None that I know of.'

McAllister noticed that Mark had pinned the deputy's badge on his ornate vest. It had been carefully polished. Mark was a dresser. McAllister tapped the badge with a finger-nail and said: 'Thanks, Mark.'

'Somebody has to watch the town while you're drifting around the countryside. How come your face ain't as pretty as usual?'

McAllister told him, omitting nothing, but not making a long story of it. The blackness of Mark's frown deepened.

'Here we go,' he said. 'I thought I'd left all this kind of thing behind me. To tell you the truth, Rem, I lost my taste for it. A man does, you know, as he matures.'

McAllister said: 'How about Stevenson? You seen him around town this morning?'

'Sure. He had breakfast at the Chinaman's. Then he visited with Lindholm at the bank.'

McAllister said: 'I'll go see Joe.' He untied the mare from the rear of the buckboard and stepped into the saddle. He sent her at a brisk clip down Main and turned her into Morrow for Joe's house. Now he knew something he had not wanted to know. There had been four men at the original hold-up. Now he was certain that there were at least five. Possibly six. Some of the gang had been here in town while four of them had stopped the stage and taken the gold. He was starting to feel nervous about that gold. The uneasy feeling that he had lost it for good was growing fast.

He rode clear round the Ramage place and saw Joe sitting on his back porch. Joe did not lift a hand in greeting, but watched him as he halted and swung down from the saddle. The girl came out of the house as he tied the mare to the picket fence.

As he approached the porch, McAllister said: 'Good morning, Miss Allison. Morning, Joe.' They no more than murmured their reply. He thought the girl looked a little scared, but he could have been wrong.

'Joe,' he said, 'neither of you look too pleased to see me. Did I do something wrong?'

'No,' the old man said. 'You didn't do nothing wrong. You're welcome, Rem.'

'I don't know what gave you that idea, sheriff,' the girl said.

'Did something happen while I was out of town?'

'Not as far as we know,' the girl said. Joe did not say a word.

'Didn't you hear about Mose Copley getting himself hurt?' McAllister asked.

'Old Mose hurt?' said Joe. 'That's bad.'

'Who is Mose Copley?' asked the girl. She was wearing a dress of a lavender colour and McAllister had never liked that colour. It was the first time there had been anything about the girl which he did not like. The rise and fall of her breasts caught his attention. She was out of breath. Had she just run from somewhere? Or was she suffering from tension?

'Mose Copley,' he told her, 'was the man I put to watching this house so that no harm should come to either of you. Somebody did their best to ruin his good looks. They also tried to crack his skull. I reckon it's most likely, all in all, that whoever did it left him for dead. Only the Mose Copley's of this world don't die so easy.'

The girl was pale. She put her hand over her mouth. 'We didn't hear or see anything,' she said.

'Maybe you didn't want to,' he said.

He turned and started back down the path. He was wasting his time here.

'Sheriff...' He stopped and turned – 'Ma'am?'

'I'm sorry about Mr Copley,' she said. He turned and walked back to them. He put a foot up on the raised porch and rested an elbow on his knee. He fixed his gaze on the old man.

'Tell me about the men who were here, Joe,' he said.

'Men?' said Joe. 'What men?

'The men who were here.'

'There wasn't no men here.'

McAllister was watching the girl now, missing nothing that she tried to conceal from her face. She was new to this kind of thing. A few more episodes of this kind and she would be hard-boiled, but she was still too soft yet. She was scared for herself and she cared in some way for Joe.

'Allison saw the men,' McAllister said. 'Didn't you, Allison?'

She tore her gaze from the old man and looked at McAllister. 'I think you've gone a little crazy, sheriff,' she said. 'I don't have any idea what you're talking about.'

'Sure,' McAllister said, 'oh, sure,' and turned to head for the white gate again. By the time he reached his horse, the girl was through the gateway and restraining him with a hand on his arm. He found that he liked her touch.

'Sheriff.' Her voice was soft. She offered the sound of it like a prayer. 'Have a thought for Uncle Joe. He's going through a hard time with the gold being stolen. He doesn't know whether he's on his head or his heels. Just leave him alone for a while.'

He looked down at her. No woman ever had more beautiful eyes.

'I'm scared for Joe all right,' he said. 'But I'm more scared for you.'

'Me?' Her surprise was genuine.

'You've got yourself into something which is way out of your depth, girl. I have a notion this is the first time for you, but I've been here a dozen times before. I know the pattern. Today, the first man was killed. I killed him. Now it all starts. Nobody will stop. Nobody'll hold back. Once the killing starts, it ain't so damn easy to stop.'

'The man you killed...'

'One of them. One of the road agents. Before we're through, there'll be another and another. Now's the time to stop it before it's too late.'

When he mentioned the killing of a road agent, he saw the stark terror in those eyes. She could control her face, but there was no controlling the eyes. They are the last thing a woman learns to control.

She got a grip on herself. She was a tough little number, and he had to admire the way she rallied.

'You talk as if I was in some way to blame,' she said.

'Prove otherwise.'

'How?'

'Tell me about the men who came to talk to Joe.'

She took her hand from his arm. 'There were no men.'

'Are you telling me that nobody came today?'

'People came, yes.'

'Such as?'

'Mr Stevenson was here.'

'Nobody else?'

'Nobody. And that's the truth.'

He patted her on the shoulder and said: 'Go give Joe a strong drink. He looks like he needs one. You most likely could use one yourself.' Then he mounted the mare and turned her away. He did not look back but sent her at a fast trot back into town.

15

Doc Robertson was coming away from Mark Tully's back room as McAllister walked into the saloon. He said: 'Rem, Bella wants to take Mose home. I have no objection, but he's going to need some good nursing. My God, I've never seen a man beaten like it. It must have been done by a madman.'

'What're Mose's chances?'

'Oh, he'll pull through – eventually. No saying what he'll be like. At the moment, he's talking fairly lucidly. He comes and goes.'

'All right if I ask him a few questions?'

'Sure. But go easy. Don't excite him at all.'

The doctor went out and McAllister went in to the back room and found Mose there with Bella and Mark Tully.

Mark kept a bed in his office and they had laid Mose on this. He was propped up on pillows. His head was bandaged heavily and the bandages covered one eye. His good eye was closed. Bella sat on the bed beside him and clung to a hand.

McAllister went and put a hand on Bella's shoulder. He said: 'Bella, it don't do any good to be sorry, but I was never more sorry than I am this minute. It was just I needed a man I could trust and I trusted Mose.'

She looked up at him coldly and said: 'That don't alter anything. Enough have happened to this poor man already. Can't nobody leave him be?'

Mose opened his eye and saw McAllister.

McAllister said: 'Mose, do you feel like talking at all?'

Bella said: 'Maybe he do and maybe he don't. But he ain't doing no talking. He going to stay still and rest up.'

'I got to tell the boss just one thing, Bella.'

'Just one is all, then.'

McAllister leaned forward to hear Mose more clearly. 'It were dark, boss. I couldn't see nothing. But I know one thing – he have a thick ring on the small finger of his right hand. He hit me with it. He were tall like you and he smell like a white woman.'

McAllister nodded. 'I got him in one, Mose. Thanks. Mark, do you have a spring wagon we can get Mose home in?'

'Leave it with me,' Mark said. Together McAllister and Tully walked out into the corridor. Tully halted and said: 'You going to catch these men, Rem?'

'Sure.'

'Only I have a liking for that black man. Anything I can do.'

'I'll need you, all right, when the time comes.'

Ten minutes later, they were gingerly carrying Mose Copley to the wagon which was drawn up alongside the loading platform behind the saloon. Lon McKenna, the mayor, found them there. The little man looked flustered and upset. He stood and looked at Mose as he lay in the wagon-bed and made disapproving noises with his tongue. When he drew McAllister aside, he said: 'The town expects results, Rem. Sure, I know some of the folks were never too partial to having a black working in town and doing well like Mose did, but he's held in high regard by a good many of us. We expect to see somebody punished for this.'

'All right, Lon. You're the justice of the peace. You back me when I do something.'

Bella drove the wagon and McAllister the buckboard. They went at a careful walking pace so that Mose would not be jogged.

Josiah Ramage, millionaire, woke in the middle of the night. He was brought from his uneasy sleep by something hard being pressed against his left temple.

As soon as he opened his eyes, he saw that his bedroom was bathed in the cold light of the moon. As he turned his head, the first thing he saw was the gun muzzle which had woken him.

A voice said: 'Stay still.'

The shape of the man seemed huge in the moonlit room. It was black and featureless. The old man was very frightened.

The man holding the gun said: 'There's no call for talk. All you have to know is the girl's been taken. We'll give you till tomorrow night to think about it. We won't hurt her till we ask you about the gold again. If we don't get the right answers then, we'll hurt her a little. Then you get another twenty-four hours, and if you don't tell us then, we'll hurt her a lot. Just bear in mind that we know all about hurting people.'

The man carefully lowered the hammer of the gun with his thumb from full-cock, put the gun away and turned for the door. Whiskey Joe slid his hand under his pillow for his own belt-gun and found that it was gone. He heard his bedroom door close quietly.

'My God,' he said as he sat up in bed. 'They've got the girl.'

He could not remember when he had been more scared.

He felt as if he wanted to retch with fear. He was cold and he shook.

What must he do?

He had friends in this town. Real friends. Men who were not bothered and fussed with his gold.

McAllister was one. Mark Tully another.

He threw his skinny old legs over the side of the bed and reached for his pants. Quickly, he dressed, stamping his feet into his boots and losing his balance in the dark. He found his gun on the bureau on the far side of the room. When he had checked the loads, he thrust the weapon away in the top of his pants. Then he searched for his old shotgun and loaded that. The weight of the weapons were a great comfort to him. He hesitated a long time in the kitchen, not daring to go out into the bright moonlight. He wondered if a stiff drink would help, but he ruled against that. He wanted his mind clear.

Suddenly, he thought: what the hell did it matter what happened to him? He was old and near the end of his days. The girl was young and just starting out. If he was killed, she need have no more financial worries. He'd made his will in her favour.

He opened the door, paused for a moment to fill his narrow chest with air, and stepped outside. Now he did not stop, but walked to the white gate and swung it open. He walked along the rear of the buildings until he came to the alleyway that would take him to the sheriff's office and hurried along it. He found the office open, but no lamp burning and nobody there.

This threw him off-balance for a moment. He had banked on McAllister being there. Or at least Charlie Stellino. Now, he crossed the street. Tully's was open. It was always open. There were three men there, propped up against the bar in wordless, drunken communion. The barkeep sat behind the bar, fast asleep. Joe leaned across the bar and poked him awake with the muzzle of the shotgun. The barkeep woke, saw the gun and snarled: 'Get that goddamn thing away from me, you old fool.'

'Old fool?' cried Joe with some of his former spirit. 'Ain't you learned nothing yet. Nobody with a million dollars is an old fool. Where's Tully?'

'Where every smart man is. Asleep.'

'In the back room?'

'What if he is?'

'Go wake him.'

'Like hell I do.'

Joe headed for the rear of the place, and the barkeep started along his side of the bar to prevent him. Joe halted and waved the shotgun. 'Keep off my tracks, you son-of-a-bitch,' he cried, 'or them drunks'll have you splattered all over 'em.'

The barkeep looked suitably horrified and halted. The old man hurried to Mark's room and inside a few seconds was prodding the saloon-owner awake.

'What the hell – !'

'You're deputy, ain't you?'

'Yes.'

'They took the girl.'

'Who took what girl?'

'Them bastards who're after my gold took the girl. Allison.'

Mark was fully awake. 'Go get yourself a drink in the bar,' he said. 'I'll be right with you.' He had started to dress before the old man was out of the room.

16

A still sleep-eyed boy, riding Mark Tully's horse, woke McAllister to tell him that he was wanted in town. When McAllister was saddling the mare, Lige, grey-faced from his bed, staggered into the barn and demanded to know if he should go along. He looked mystified when McAllister said, no, he dared not use any more Copleys. The town boy did not know why McAllister was wanted, but he said Mr Tully was fussing some. The boy had gathered from Mr Tully that it was about 'some goddamn girl'.

McAllister galloped into town and tied up outside the saloon. Mark Tully was in the bar drinking black coffee and old Joe was flushed with whiskey.

Mark said: 'They took the girl, Rem.'

'Did they say why?'

Joe said: 'They want to know where my claim is.'

McAllister poured himself some coffee and stared at the barkeep, who was sitting upright behind the bar, fast asleep. Three drunks stood at the bar, leaning and not moving.

McAllister said: 'I ain't worried two cents worth of cold piss.'

Joe said: 'Well, I'm worried to hell, and if you know what's good for you, you'll start worrying, McAllister. I'm not just any old citizen. I'm Joe Ramage and I'm worth a million. If I'm worried, everybody else has to be worried.'

'Joe,' said McAllister, 'you're losing faith. Just sit around till the stage gets in and all will be revealed.'

Mark finished a cup of coffee, poured himself another and said: 'You're taking this very calmly. I thought you thought a lot of that girl.'

'Sure,' said McAllister, 'I think she's one hell of a girl. But I ain't fazed.'

He drank his cup of coffee, settled himself in a corner in a chair, put his feet on another chair and went to sleep. Joe said: 'He's getting too damn old for the job, he did ought to be replaced by a younger and more able man.'

'I don't know,' said Mark, though there was doubt in his voice. 'I reckon the bastard is about to play his hole card.'

The old man said: 'It had better be good, or I'll have his guts for galluses. The thought of that girl...'

They were all there on the sidewalk when the stage got in, Horry Wanlace up, grinning, whip in hand. The first passenger out of the vehicle was Charlie Stellino. He moved stiffly and in evident pain. His grin was glassy and inclined to be fixed.

'Don't pretend I ain't a surprise, McAllister,' he said, 'because I know I am. I bet you told these fellers I was out of the fight. All washed up.'

McAllister told him coldly: 'Your name just naturally didn't crop up.'

Charlie looked hurt. He turned to hand somebody down from the stage. This was a tall and extremely fine-looking girl. One of those women who, without the aid of any kind of artifice or chemistry, are able to turn men's heads and bowl them over. On the face of it, she had a number of things going against her physically, but the general effect was stunning. She was too tall, for a start, and very tall women were not admired at that time. The nose was a mite too long. The mouth a shade too wide. The hands possibly a fraction too long. The figure a suggestion too pronounced. The whole made up a young woman who immediately attracted men to her. There was about her, in spite of old and made-over clothes of rather unfashionable cut, in spite of having been confined to stage coaches for days and even nights, an air of cool elegance that stole away the masculine breath. In spite of the male stares and being in a strange town, she was as self-possessed as a princess among her subjects. Men had already started to drag their hats from their heads.

McAllister stepped forward. 'Miss Disart?' She smiled. 'You must be Sheriff McAllister, sir.'

McAllister bowed, and she gave him a long, cool hand, at the same time turning to smile at the others and waiting for them to be introduced. McAllister named names, and she said a kind word to all of them, not forgetting the boy who had ridden to wake McAllister from his sleep. She was even polite to the three drunks who had roused themselves from the bar at the announcement of female loveliness on the morning stage.

Old Horry Wanlace hovered, declaring: 'I take treasure out and I bring treasure in.'

Somebody said: 'Just as well you didn't lose this one, Horry.'

Joe Ramage said: 'I don't get it. How can this young lady be – ' Then he got it and gazed in wonderment and distress from McAllister to the girl. 'McAllister, you knowed this all along. By crackey, you ain't telling me – '

'Yes, Joe,' said McAllister. 'That's what I'm telling you. That's why I wasn't worried. They planted the girl on you. What do you think of this one for a replacement.'

Joe said: 'Can this one cook?'

The young lady said, in a voice that struck them all of a heap: 'I don't think you'll have any complaints on that score, Uncle Joe.'

Charlie Stellino stood on the sidelines and fumed, unable to believe that his re-entry into town had not caused a sensation.

'I bet,' he said, desperately trying to gain McAllister's attention. 'you didn't think to see me for a month or more.'

'A man,' said McAllister, 'lives in hope. Charlie, you came back at the right time. I want you to stay with Joe and never let him out of your sight. That goes for the girl, too.'

Charlie said: 'That don't call for agony.'

'It could be dangerous, so keep your gun by you.'

'You realise you're getting a hero on the cheap?'

Lennie Wallach, the newspaperman, came across the street from his office and wanted to know if there was anything he could do. Which meant, did McAllister have anything for his rag? McAllister said, no, but he would have something for Lennie before the morning was through.

He arranged for Joe Ramage and his new niece to take a room at the hotel. He wanted them both where there were plenty of people. Colonel English found them two connecting rooms on his third floor. Charlie installed himself in Joe's room. The only access to the rooms was along a wide corridor. Joe went there meekly enough, still puzzled and bewildered and not knowing whether to accept this new girl as his niece. He had, he said, become mighty fond of the other one and it was not easy at his age to switch affections at the drop of a hat.

McAllister questioned the colonel about his guest Stevenson. There was no mystery. Mr Stevenson had checked out yesterday afternoon. Did the colonel have any idea where he had gone? Unhelpfully, the colonel suggested that he most likely had gone to fetch his horse from the livery.

At the livery stable, Lon McKenna's boy, Tommy Shultz, said that Mr Stevenson had taken his own horse and hired another from the livery. He had tied his portmanty on the spare horse. The boy did not know who the spare horse was for.

In reply to the question: had anybody else ridden out yesterday, the boy told him that Mr Madders had gone out on his own horse during the evening and had not been back. He owed five dollars on his feed bill. Nobody else had taken a horse from the livery yesterday.

McAllister walked down to the bank. He found that the banker was apparently quite well-informed about the recent happenings in town. He even knew about Charlie Stellino being wounded.

'I cannot say, sheriff, that I am best pleased,' Lindholm said. 'You gave me an assurance that the gold shipment was safe. This is a serious catastrophe, you know. I shall have to take Mr Ramage's advice on how to proceed from here on in.'

McAllister was not quite sure what he meant by that. He pushed a question or two at Lindholm. 'Did Stevenson call in here before he left town?'

'Stevenson? Left town?' The banker sounded quite startled.

'Yes,' McAllister told him. 'He lit out with Madders and the girl.'

'Madders. Who is Madders? And what girl?'

'Madders is the man who came into town and pretended to have no connection with Stevenson.'

'I'm afraid I don't begin to understand.' This was one moment when the banker came near to giving himself away in panic. It caught him unawares and he did not know what to do with it.

'The girl was the one the gold thieves planted on Whiskey Joe as his niece.'

'My God, McAllister,' cried Lindholm, 'this is the kind of nonsense one reads about in dime novels. You can hardly expect an intelligent man – '

'What did Stevenson and you talk about when he was here in this office?'

'I beg your pardon.'

Lindholm looked scandalised, horrified, unbelieving that he had been asked the question.

Lindholm, this thing is going to blow up in our faces. A deputy has been wounded and a man killed.'

That shook Lindholm. 'A man killed? Who? I didn't hear of a man being killed.'

'One of the stage robbers ran into a bullet.'

'Whose bullet?'

'Mine.'

The banker seemed to gaze at McAllister in awe. 'This is terrible,' he said. 'That this should happen in a peaceful country. Sheriff, are you quite sure you're on top of this thing?'

'Not yet I ain't. But I will be. Just as soon as I find out who the road agents have inside this town working with them.'

'You don't mean to suggest – '

'Yes, sir, that's what I do mean to suggest.'

'It is absolutely unthinkable that – '

'Where do you reckon the road agents are taking the gold, Lindholm?'

'Taking the gold? My word, how would I know a thing like that?'

As McAllister walked out through the bank, he winked at Ham Stoppard, who gaped back at him. He was still gaping when Lindholm snapped irritably from his office door: 'Stoppard, come in here.'

Lindholm stood there, bitterly regretting that he had overruled Stevenson's plan to take the gold in Casper on the grounds that it was too dangerous and might lead to shooting. Fear swooped through him and he fought to suppress it.

17

A passenger on the stage who had received no attention from anybody was a small man named Pudsy Harper. His birth certificate said William Ditch Harper, but who remembers what is written on a birth certificate? Pudsy was an inhabitant of the slums of Chicago and, as such, considered himself a cut above the hicks around him who called themselves Westerners even though they had not been here a minute. To him, they talked funny, they acted funny and worst of all they were slow.

Even this man McAllister who had hired him to come here seemed mighty slow in making up his mind about anything. He seemed to ponder each reply demanded of him for five minutes at a time. Though a crook in birth and rearing, Pudsy was a real get-up-and-go man. A great believer in the American virtue of enterprise and action. 'If you don't get up and do it fast, some other son-of-a-bitch will,' he would say as his contribution to world wisdom.

He was small, quick-moving as a ferret, alternately pathetic and dangerous. He had been a dip as a boy, living by picking the pockets of the more affluent of his fellows. From there, he had graduated to plain burglary. Finally, he had learned the trade of a peterman in the pen, where all good men learn their trades. As a safebreaker, he had never been caught. Jail had taught him much, amongst which was the fact that it is better to be careful than sorry. He never tackled a job beyond his capability and he never tackled one which was not as safe as any such job could be.

This one, here in this hick town, he reckoned was a pushover. He had the protection and patronage of the local sheriff. You could not do better than that. He had to confess that the business intrigued him, for it looked as if the whole town was in on this caper, except the man who was being robbed. The sheriff had hinted that even the mayor knew what was going on. It was hard to believe, but McAllister did not look like a liar to him. The man was too damn simple for that.

He lay on his bed in the best hotel in town. On that he had insisted. The best. He thought about the job. McAllister had described the safe to him and told him the name of the maker.

'I could open it with my fingers,' Pudsy had told the sheriff. 'I wouldn't like you to think I couldn't. But that'd take time. If you want a quick job, I'll have to blow it. There'll be quite a noise and it'll be heard.'

That worried the sheriff a bit, but he said if noise was necessary then they would have to put up with it. What did Pudsy need? Pudsy told him. It would all be at the bank when Pudsy arrived there to do the job. When would that be? Pudsy wanted to know.

The sheriff said: 'You just be available when I want you. We'll get you into the bank when the time's right.'

Pudsy said: 'All right.' But he did not know that he liked the idea of kicking his heels waiting on the word of another man. In a way, being a safe-breaker was something like being an artist; there was temperament to be considered. He felt himself getting a little nervous. The feeling came quite unaccountably and he did not like it.

'I hope the safe is just exactly as you described it to me,' he said. 'I mean, my craft is kind of exact and all that, you know. I mean, just a few things different and it could all go wrong. Blowing a safe ain't child's play, you know.'

McAllister said: 'You want to change your mind, now's the time to do it. We'll call it a day and I'll see you out of town. I daresay I might find something to arrest you for, though. Like vagrancy. Or maybe even rape. The preacher's daughter, say. That would kind of rile up the local populace.'

Pudsy did not like the sound of that. He took a good look at the sheriff and wondered if he was a simple hick after all.

'Just so's you don't keep me hanging around in this lousy hotel room too long,' he said.

The sheriff gave him a doubtful look and left the room. Pudsy found a pack of cards in his grip and played a little patience to calm his nerves. Calm his nerves? My God, he thought, what had gotten into him? He hadn't suffered from nerves ever before in all his life. Maybe it was being among all these cowboys. They were sure a funny lot.

He was having a tough time getting the game to come out right and he was starting to cheat when the sheriff returned. He came so quietly, he was at Pudsy's elbow before Pudsy even knew he was in the room.

'Jesus Christ', said the safe-breaker, 'you scared me out of my life almost. Do you have to creep up on a feller that way?'

'The quieter, the better,' said the sheriff, 'for a chore like this.'

Pudsy saw that the man had on a pair of Indian shoes that were much like slippers. He himself wore a pair of shoes with india-rubber soles, but they were noisy compared with those worn by this cat-footed sheriff. McAllister said: 'Go down onto the street and turn right. Go along a half-block and you'll find an alleyway there. Go down the alleyway and you'll find a man waiting there for you. He'll get you into the rear of the bank. He has all your gear with him.'

'How do I know—' Pudsy began.

The sheriff interrupted him with: 'It's too late for questions or doubts. Just do it. Hear? Count to fifty before you go.' He turned and walked out of the room.

Pudsy counted to fifty. The fact that he did so obediently made him a little mad. This was the last time he worked with a bunch of dumb hicks. What the hell kind of a town was it where the mayor and the sheriff were in on a bank job?

When he reached fifty, he walked out of his room and down the stairs. The street was almost deserted when he walked out onto it. Just to prove itself a one-horse town, there were no street lights of any kind. The darkness of the street was cut here and there by a few lights from houses. The lights of Tully's saloon threw quite a large bright arc. The bank stood in total darkness.

He found the deep, dark maw of the alleyway and hesitated for a moment as he found that he could not see a yard in front of him down there. For a moment, this quiet cow-town was menacing to the city dweller. He called himself a goddam fool and pushed forward into the darkness. He had taken no more than thirty paces when he heard a soft whistle off to his left. Halting, he heard a man say: 'Harper?'

'Yeah.'

'Over here.'

He stepped to the side of the alleyway and saw a faint gleam of light ahead. A man said: 'Go ahead to the light.' Pudsy went forward cautiously, now and then stumbling on uneven ground. Then he had stepped through an open doorway and he heard the door close behind him. Now, another door opened ahead and he walked into a large lighted room. He realised that this was the main part of the bank. Off to his left was a smaller room. At his elbow, a voice said: 'There's the safe, Harper. Go ahead.' He knew the sheriff was there with him.

He walked into the smaller office and saw the Purely Crutten safe in the far corner. A lamp gleamed on the desk in the centre. All the gear he had requested was laid out neatly on the desk. He stepped forward to check it and saw to his relief and pleasure that everything he had asked for was there. This gave him a sudden burst of confidence. Maybe people who could be as efficient as this were not hopeless amateurs after all.

The sheriff said: 'Everything there you want?'

'Sure.'

'Then for God's sake hurry it up.'

Pudsy Harper rubbed his hands together and got to work. He could feel the old professional excitement rising in him. That kind of excitement never threw him, only inspired him to do his best work.

He worked smoothly and with skill. Everything seemed to be in order. It was only when he opened up the powder bags and ran the powder through his fingers, as he always did before using it, that he noticed something wrong.

18

The last place anybody would have thought of looking for the stage robbers was in the house of the bank owner. J. Howard Lindholm was, to start with, a man wholly above suspicion. By the evening of the bank raid, Lindholm started to undergo a curious transformation of character. Or maybe it was that he had discovered things about himself of which he had been ignorant in the past. For example, his original plan to obtain Whiskey Joe's gold had originated in his need for money, his desire to be rich and to fulfil his ambitions. His devotion to his own cause may have been quite passionate, but the carrying out of the scheme had been a cold and calculated process of thought inside his skull. Now, however, he found that he was obtaining excitement from the carrying out of the scheme itself. More than that, it fed his vanity and pride.

There was the girl. A few months ago, even a week or two before, such a woman would have been beyond his dreams. He had never been much of a hand with women and he had never fooled himself that he was any oil painting. Now, here was the girl smiling at him.

He had discovered her through the use of a private investigator in Chicago. Her real name was Carla Blount. Not much of a name for a beautiful girl, but there it was. She had come to town as Allison Disart and she had fooled old Joe into thinking her his niece. That had not been difficult. She had spent five years on the stage and she had at one time been the room-mate of the Disart girl. She had been made for this part.

He looked at her sitting on the edge of the bed, brushing her hair. The lamplight shone on its glossy darkness. To think that so much loveliness was his for the taking, somehow caught him by the throat. He wondered if a man could stand only so much happiness. When she turned her head to smile at him, he found something there he had not expected, a friendly warmth, even affection. That was almost too much for him.

He didn't fool himself. Behind all the present excitement and expectancy, his brain stayed cool. He knew the main attraction was the gold. The girl was sensible. She had herself to think of. Yet, as he knew, money could evoke real passion in a certain kind of woman. Nor did the gold prevent her having a genuine liking for him. After all, he had made himself as charming as possible to her.

'Howard,' she said, 'what will you do when this is all over?'

He took off his necktie and loosened his shirt collar. 'I thought I knew, my dear,' he said, 'but now I'm not so sure. I had thought of England or Ireland for a few years. Some wise investments. You know the kind of thing.'

She laughed. 'Sensible, but dull,' she said.

He smiled in an avuncular kind of a way. 'That's my present thought. Investment, sure. That looks after the future. But I think maybe a year or two of fun. I could afford it.'

She laid down her brush and threw the dark veil of her hair back from her face.

'Hank Stevenson wants me to go to South America with him,' she said. 'Unbutton me at the back, please.'

He went across the room to her and started to unbutton her dress. As his fingers touched her neck, a thrill that was like a deep shudder ran through him. Her scent touched his nostrils and he was painfully conscious that it was too long since he had had a woman.

'Stevenson,' he said. 'I didn't know, it was like –'

'It isn't,' she said. 'Not yet. I guess he scares me a little. He acts and talks like a gentleman, but I've heard the other men talking.'

'Stevenson a gentleman?' Lindholm said. 'The man's a blackguard with blood on his hands. I would hate to think of you... You can do better than that, my dear.'

'A girl has to think of her future.'

Their gazes met in the mirror. He did not look at his best

with his jacket off and his shirt unbuttoned. As he unbuttoned her dress, she slipped it down, and now he could see the creamy rounds of her breasts and the delicious divide between them. The sight almost made him faint.

'Carla,' he said, 'I'm an old man to you, I guess.'

She turned and looked up at him, giving him the full benefit of those eyes, as if he was not devastated enough.

'You're mature, Howard,' she said. 'I don't feel you're old at all.'

'That's nice of you.'

'I feel so safe with you. Just having you here. I've led a pillar-to-post kind of a life. I'd so much love to settle down.'

'My dear,' he said, and was so overcome at what was being offered to him, when he had only contemplated the possibility of a night or two in her company, that he bent down and put his lips to her shoulder where it sloped up to her long slender neck. She put an arm around his neck. Then she stood up and his arms were around her, holding her tightly against him. He kissed her on the mouth, and then he went a little wild and she had to tear herself away from him. She panted nicely like a modest woman overcome by unseemly but delicious passion.

'Hurry,' she said, 'I can't wait.'

J. Howard Lindholm needed no second bidding, as they say. He had ever been a man for instant action when it was called for and he had never heard it called for so urgently as now. With a speed that would have done credit to an equally aroused man of half his age, he began to tear his clothes from him. His frenzy of speed dispensed with pants, shirt, socks, in no time at all, while the young lady was still struggling with all the female appendages and restrictions of the period. He saw, with his usual insight, that he would reach the post first to no avail, if he did not go to her assistance. With fumbling fingers he unlaced and pulled. In no time at all, it seemed, he had the young lady stark and incredibly beautiful upon the bed, hurling himself upon her with an enthusiasm which did him credit.

It was at that very moment that a block down the street, Pudsy Harper blew the bank safe.

19

The robbery of the Black Horse bank was a strange incident in the life of the town from many aspects.

For one thing, there were a great many people involved in it. There was no member, for example, of Mark Tully's backroom club who was not fully aware of what was going on. This meant the mayor, who was the senior justice of the peace, and two councilmen. The explosive which Pudsy used and which was, as you might say, provided by the town, had been obtained by a friend of a cousin of the mayor who worked in mining. This was because the local gunsmith, who had a good store of explosives, was not in on the plot. McAllister had ruled against his inclusion, because he was known to be a friend of J. Howard Lindholm.

This explosive did not arrive until the eleventh hour; indeed McAllister nearly suffered heart-failure, it was delayed so long. Eventually, on the night of the bank raid, it arrived in a mine wagon. Everybody concerned was so relieved that it had arrived that nobody thought to check whether it was the normal powder the average cow-country man would think to use. None of them knowing anything about the latest developments in the explosives industry, which about that time was great, they thought there could be little difference between one type and another. Unbelievable, maybe, but true nonetheless.

It must be said in poor Pudsy's honour that he tried to back out at the last moment. Nobody in his right mind, he claimed not without justification, would use an explosive he did not know something about. Not for this kind of job in a confined space. These wretched hicks showed not the slightest interest in his right and proper feelings. Every one of them over-ruled him. Now they had come thus far in the robbing of their own bank, there was no turning back for them. They left Pudsy no choice – they stood between him and the door with drawn guns. Guns had always terrified Pudsy.

In all fairness to the man, we must recognise that under the circumstances it was understandable that by the time he came to setting his charges, the little man from Chicago was confused. Working with an unknown material, he was faced with a gamble – whether to underestimate the charge used or to be generous with it. He argued, quite falsely it turned out, that nothing new was better than the old. Ergo: new explosive must be weaker than good old black powder. So he was lavish with the unknown material and, did he but know it, laid charges which, placed strategically, would have been enough to blow the bank itself across the nearby creek.

For safety's sake, he had placed the mattress from Lindholm's office bed across the front of the safe with a couple of chairs to hold it in place. He then ran a fuse from the inner to the outer office. Before he struck his match and ignited the fuse, he remarked with the casualness that he thought marked the true professional: 'This is liable to make quite a bang, sheriff. My advice is get your head down.'

McAllister dropped to one knee and cupped his head in his arms, saying: 'Go ahead.' He called to anybody who was near that the safe was about to be blown. Pudsy struck his match and the fuse started to splutter. He and McAllister watched the burn race along the fuse line and enter the inner office. At this point some ultimate truth seemed to strike the little safe-breaker. He was heard to utter: 'Oh, my Gawd,' and McAllister saw him start in a sudden rush of panic for the rear door of the bank.

He never reached it.

As he passed the bank counter where each day Ham Stoppard did his daily stint, there came a stunning volume of sound and every particle of solid matter and of air seemed to be rent and shattered from its original form. Pudsy Harper's lightweight self was ripped from its feet and hurled with a horrifyingly titanic power into the outer darkness. McAllister, crouching near the street door of the bank, felt himself being hurled backwards as if he weighed no more than a morsel of paper, smashed through the door itself and thrown violently onto the street.

The force of the explosion must have knocked him unconscious, but how long he lay there in the dust of the street he would never know. All he knew as he staggered trembling to his feet was that his whole being was shattered. All around him there seemed to be wreckage, confusion and flame. Men shouted. One stumbled into McAllister. Through the chaos and confusion of that moment, McAllister retained the importance of obtaining the gold. He seized the man who had stumbled into him and found that it was Lon McKenna, the mayor. He shouted into Lon's face: 'Get the gold.'

'Gold?' said McKenna, wonderingly.

McAllister turned the mayor into the wreckage of the bank and shoved him forward. 'Get the gold.'

McAllister himself must have been light-headed. He was vaguely conscious of knocking out some flames which were licking at the tails of his coat. He then carefully walked through the frame of the doorway, ignoring the fact that the walls of the bank were no longer there. By the bright light of the flames, his astonished eyes saw that the banker's desk had been transferred from the small office into the larger one where it rested in a rather forlorn condition on top of the tellers' counter.

A ghost of a creature appeared in front of McAllister, apparently carefully dressed in rags, his face looking like that of a Kentucky minstrel wearing a silly and inane grin.

'Who the hell're you?' McAllister demanded.

'Tully,' was the reply. 'Who the hell're you?'

'McAllister. Get the goddam gold.'

Together, they staggered on failing legs in the direction of the safe. When they found it, they stood and gazed in consternation and dismay. While everything around it had been destroyed, the giant safe stood there in almost pristine condition.

Tully said a very socially unacceptable word. They approached and found that the safe was too hot to touch. They both said: 'Ouch.'

'We got to get the gold,' said McAllister.

Out on the street somebody was yelling: 'Somebody's blown up the bank. The bank's been robbed. The bank's been robbed.'

McAllister told Tully: 'Get the gold, for God's sake, while I head off the local citizenry.' He drew his pistol and tottered out onto the street, bawling as loudly as he could: 'There they go. After 'em, boys,' and fired several shots in the direction of the creek.

A man came up to him and said: 'Hold hard, man. I don't see anybody.'

'Ah,' said McAllister, 'you ain't trained to it like me.'

'Who the hell're you?' the man demanded.

'McAllister,' McAllister snarled. 'Get a posse together. They went over the creek.'

'Like hell they went over the creek. Nobody didn't go over no creek.'

'You calling me a liar, you son-of-a-bitch?' McAllister demanded.

'Sure I am calling you a liar. You are a liar.'

'You're under arrest,' said McAllister.

'What for?'

'Calling the law a liar. You can't go around calling the law a liar at a time like this.' He turned to a nearby man, who stood gaping this way and that with a gun in his hand. 'Arrest this man.'

The man said: 'This is old Billy Dyson, I can't arrest him.'

'Go ahead and arrest him. He's a bank robber.'

'Is that a fact? This world will never cease to surprise me.' He turned his gun on Dyson. 'Ain't there no honest man left anywhere? Come along, Dyson, you thieving son-of-a-bitch.'

'I ain't no bank robber,' said Dyson, 'and you know it,' scared out of his wits by the pointed gun which he knew to be hair-triggered.

'Tell that to the judge,' said his arrester.

'Good man,' said McAllister and ran back through the flames.

He found that Mark Tully had the back of the safe off.

'Blast is a funny thing, ain't it?' said Mark. Considering the physical condition he was in and ignoring the fact that he showed an inclination to walk around in circles, Mark was being his usual efficient self. He had a small pile of canvas sacks there, ready for the gold. Now he rapidly began to put the pokes of gold from the safe into the sacks. McAllister ran them to the rear of the building, where the distraught mayor seemed amazed to see any gold at all. He staggered away down an alley under the great weight. When McAllister got back into the bank, he found Mark arguing fiercely with a man who was demanding to know what was going on here. He was Smith, owner of a hardware store in town. He was an anti-committee man and was suspicious of anything. McAllister bustled him out onto the street, telling him that if he received an injury the county could not be responsible.

'That man was stealing gold in there,' Smith accused.

'No, sir,' said McAllister stoutly, but with failing courage, 'he's trying to save what's left. Why ain't you out after the thieves?'

'Thieves?' What thieves?'

'The ones who blew up the bank and lit off across the creek with the gold.'

'Say, is that a fact?'

'True bill.'

There was no further chance to continue this conversation, for a wild figure came cantering down the street like an obscene Percheron. McAllister, with some difficulty, recognised the owner of the bank, J. Howard Lindholm. This gentleman, clad in longjohns and an expression of frozen horror halted and gazed at the meagre remains of his bank.

'Disaster,' he said.

McAllister could almost feel sorry for him. 'We're saving what we can,' said McAllister, 'at some danger to life, I might say.'

'The gold,' said Lindholm, turning a crazed pair of eyes on the sheriff.

'A gang of four men was seen escaping from the fire,' McAllister told him, lying desperately. 'They were carrying sacks which we guessed contained the gold you speak of. What gold was this, Lindholm?'

'Gold?' Lindholm seemed to come a little closer from a long way off. But as yet he was not really a part of the scene. 'Gold?'

'What gold do you refer to? I thought all the gold had been shipped out.'

Lindholm's eyes began to come back into focus. 'Ah,' he said, eyes wary and scared, 'we always keep some gold at the bank. Naturally. It would be that the thieves were after. Did you get clear sight of them, McAllister?'

'Their leader was a tall man, dressed in grey and riding a sorrel horse. I've seen him some place, but I'm damned if I can place him. The other was a dark fellow with a scar down his right cheek.'

'My God,' cried the banker, quite taken off balance and scarcely knowing what he was saying: 'Stevenson and Cutter.'

McAllister gave a glad cry. 'That's them. I'm grateful, Lindholm. I would have placed them eventually. But, say, you'll catch your death dressed like that.'

Lindholm looked down at himself. 'I must get in there and save what I can,' he said.

'Everything's being done,' McAllister said. 'You know who your friends are at a time like this. There's neighbours of yours in there risking life and limb on your behalf.'

Lindholm swallowed. 'I'm grateful.'

Ham Stoppard loped up and gazed mournfully on the burning remnants of the bank.

'Oh, my God, Mr Lindholm, sir,' he said. 'Everything's gone.'

'Everything,' said Lindholm.

Ham began to make a strange noise. McAllister could not tell if he was laughing or crying.

McAllister said: 'Take Mr Lindholm home, Ham. We'll clear up here.'

Five or six horsemen clattered down the street. Two of them were almost too drunk to stay in the saddle. McAllister gathered that they thought they were chasing Indians. Ham Stoppard took Lindholm away. The banker was saying over and over: 'I'm finished, Ham, I'm all washed up.'

'Looks like it, Mr Lindholm, sir,' said Ham, a shade too cheerfully, Lindholm thought.

20

They put the gold under the hay in Lon McKenna's big barn without a guard. The gold and money which did not belong to Whiskey Joe they carried to Lindholm's house and handed over to the banker. Lindholm was dressed and he looked like hell, haggard and old. He must have drunk a half-bottle of whiskey since they last saw him. He couldn't check what was there because there were no books to check it against. He still apparently had a few of his wits about him.

He said to Mark Tully, McAllister and the few others who toted the safe's contents to his house: 'Doesn't it strike you as strange that the thieves only took gold and not money?'

They all agreed they thought that was strange.

When they had gone and Lindholm went into his room to find the girl, he said to her: 'Carla, there's something mighty odd here. All those thieves took was Joe's gold. Everything else seems to be intact.'

'McAllister described Stevenson to you, Howard,' the girl said. 'Do you think it's at all possible Stevenson did rob the bank?'

'After tonight I'd believe anything was possible.' He looked at her searchingly. 'Does this mean you and I have no future together?'

'You must think me a pretty shallow sort of creature, Howard. I'm not the kind of girl to desert a man just because he's down.'

That was just what he had thought. Now he said: 'Does that mean you care a little for me for myself?'

She smiled cutely. 'Sure, I do, but I'm not forgetting either that Joe has plenty more gold where that came from.'

He gazed at her, wonderingly. 'You're some girl, Carla. You really mean that, don't you? You mean for us to go after Joe's claim.'

She came and sat beside him on the bed. She had not dressed, only covered her nakedness with a thin silk dressing-gown. He could see the faint lines of her breasts, and they told him that paradise was still there for the taking. He was so grateful to her for this saving hand that he put an arm around her and kissed her on the cheek.

'I guess,' he said, 'with you and me together, anything can be done.'

She kissed him back with a show of real affection. 'Howard, we'll be rich yet.'

'I'm not really the man to ride the mountains hunting up a gold claim, my darling.'

She showed her strong white teeth. 'You and me are not going to stir from this town, Howard. Remember, you're still old Joe's adviser and friend. I know you can persuade the old fool to tell you where the claim is. Then you start using Stevenson. I don't care if he stole the gold or not. He's greedy and he'll go after the mine. We have to fix it that he brings the gold to you. Or even a percentage of the gold.'

He struck a fist into a palm. Here he saw difficulties. 'But can it be done?'

'You're forgetting. Between us, we can do anything.'

He saw it all then, like an inspiration. This night was not the end for him. It was a beginning. He could pull off his coup after all. He would have money and this woman.

He laughed and pulled her back onto the bed, quite deftly opening the front of her dressing gown as he did so.

'How's this for starters?' he said, and she giggled delightfully.

21

This was not the end of Josiah Ramage's troubles, and nobody knew it better than McAllister. But first things first. Two of his people had been injured in the brand new millionaire's service and he must pay for the fact. A millionaire's values are money, and it is as well to recognise the fact, if only out of courtesy to him.

McAllister washed and shaved in his office and walked around to Joe's for breakfast.

'By the great horned toad, McAllister,' cried the millionaire, jumping a little on his chair, 'what in hell's going on around here?' He could see with interest the black rims around the sheriff's eyes where he had failed to remove the remains of the burned black powder from the explosion. 'How much was taken from the bank? Did they catch any of the thieves?'

'None of the bank's cash was taken,' McAllister replied. 'Only your gold.'

Joe wrung his hands a little. The real Allison Disart sat there and looked at McAllister with an expression on her face commonly worn by young women when they are not quite sure what kind of a fellow a man is. Then she turned her attention, maybe a mite reluctantly, to her new-found uncle, who seemed to be on the brink of openly weeping. A distressing fact in a land where only women and Mexicans were expected to weep. In a voice all broken up with emotion, Joe said: 'My God, this is terrible. What's the country coming to? Huh? Can you tell me that? When an honest gold prospector can't put his hard-won gold in a safe place?'

'Calm down, Joe,' McAllister said. 'Your gold's as safe as it ever was.'

'Safe?' whined the millionaire (for, as you see, wealth makes cowards of us all). 'How in tarnation can it be safe if it's stole?'

'It's safe in my keeping.'

Joe was on his feet, knotted forefinger pointing quiveringly at the sheriff. 'If that's supposed to be a comfort to me, you got another think coming.'

'You ungrateful old – man,' said McAllister, out of deference to the feminine company and the manners of his period, which forbade naughty words in front of what was called the 'gentle sex'. 'Half this town went out last night and blew the bank to – ah – kingdom come and risked their necks and reputations to save your fool gold.'

'Where's it at right now?' quavered poor old Joe.

'Under the hay in the mayor's barn.'

The millionaire went white. 'I wouldn't trust that thieving son-of-a-bitch as far as I could throw a goddam pyeanny.'

'Lady present,' said McAllister.

'Don't mind me,' said Allison.

Joe did not. 'You get that gold in here's fast's you can rustle yourself, McAllister,' he cried.

McAllister was firm. 'Get a grip on yourself, Joe. You're

talking wild. Everybody's been working to save your gold and your life. We put you and your gold together and you're asking for trouble. No, we keep the gold for you, and if you have any sense at all, you'll pack your grips and take Miss Allison and yourself clean out of the country to some safe place.'

'Like hell I do.'

'I can't guard you twenty-four hours a day.'

'You couldn't guard a goddam hen-house from coyotes.'

After that, their conversation became somewhat heated and McAllister could sincerely wish that he had kept his mouth shut and allowed the old man to believe that his gold had been stolen by persons unknown. He checked that there was somebody guarding the gold in the livery, had Charlie Stellino help him tote the gold over to his office and put it in a box which stood in plain sight of anybody who cared to view it. Charlie said he might as well go out on Main and hand it around to the worthy citizens. McAllister rode out to his place to take a look at Mose Copley.

Mose was looking pretty sorry for himself. He had every right to. But he was cheerful enough. That could not be said of Bella Copley, who acted as if she owed McAllister a pretty bitter grudge. And he could not blame her for that. She was right. This was none of Mose's affair and McAllister should have left him out of it.

The blacksmith knew what was in McAllister's mind. 'Don't you pay no heed to Bella now, boss. She get over it.' Mose sat on the stoop and smoked his corn-cob pipe. 'I watching that trail yonder. Soon or late, one of the men you want is going to ride along there. Stands to reason. When I see him, you're going to know.'

McAllister found Bella in the kitchen of his house, baking bread. 'Bella, I suppose it ain't no good saying I'm sorry.'

'No, it ain't,' she said. 'I'm mad and I aim to stay mad.' So he got out of there and watched young Lige working a green horse in the circular pen. After a while, the boy dismounted and tied the horse to the snubbing post. He sauntered his lank form across the pen to McAllister and grinned. He said: 'I reckon my old lady sure gave you hell in there, boss.'

McAllister wanted to wipe that grin off his face. 'You go to hell,' he said, and went and saddled his mare. He reckoned he had had just about enough of humanity. He rode back to town, unaware of the truth that men are blissful in their misery. Humanity had a good deal more in store for him.

That night, two horsemen rode quietly into the thickets which lay north of town, dismounted, tied their horses and quietly walked the remainder of their way. They used shadow to its full advantage and came by the rear way to the house of J. Howard Lindholm. One man tapped on the kitchen door with the butt of his quirt, and they waited. Then he tapped again, and a moment later the door opened and showed them a darkened room. They stepped past him and, guided by the light from the hall, walked to the rear parlour of the house. The man who had admitted them shut and locked the kitchen door and followed them.

Sitting in the parlour, they found the girl who had impersonated Allison Disart. She ignored the smaller of the two men, but found a smile for the taller of the two.

Henry Holst Stevenson bowed. He looked very different now from the man who had surveyed the Black Horse street from the bank window. He was dressed in a blue hickory shirt and mackinaw coat, with striped California pants tucked into knee-high boots. The gun at his right hip had a used looked to it. His old hat had seen years of service.

His companion was dressed in levis and chaps. In the crook of his left arm he carried a short repeating carbine. He was young and looked harmless; both were his stock-in-trade. He had played on them for years. He had been the greenhorn in Mark Tully's back room. His name was Wallace Harms, but it was a long time since he had been called anything but the Kid.

Stevenson was saying: 'It's nice to see you, Carla. It's always nice to see a beautiful woman.' He would have followed this with the usual flow of nonsense he produced for any woman, but the banker came bustling into the room and at once turned on him fiercely.

'Well, Hank, this is a fine kettle of fish. My God, have you gone out of your mind? The bank is a total wreck. You must be crazy to do a thing like this without consulting me. I am angry. I am very angry.'

The other two looked at him in astonishment.

Stevenson said: 'J. Howard, I do not have the remotest idea what you're talking about.' He turned to the girl. 'What the hell's he talking about, Carla?'

The banker spluttered: 'Don't know what I'm talking about? My God, I never want to live through the last day again.' He looked from one face to the other. 'You mean – you mean you honestly don't . . . '

The girl said: 'Somebody blew the bank up.' She could not help laughing. 'It don't bear thinking on.'

Lindholm said: 'The bank was blown up and nothing was taken except Joe Ramage's gold.'

Now Stevenson and the Kid looked at each other.

Stevenson said: 'This smells to high heaven.' He stood there, thinking, his heavy chin resting on his powerful chest. He slowly raised his head and stared at them. He said in a slow thoughtful voice: 'This is the point where everything starts to fall to pieces around us. If we don't get a right grasp on it.'

Lindholm said: 'Just what do you –'

'Didn't you hear Jim Barker was shot?'

The banker's voice rose to falsetto. 'Barker shot? Oh, my God.'

The girl said: 'Who did it?'

Stevenson said: 'We don't know for sure who did it. Nobody saw it. I think it has to be McAllister.'

Lindholm was doing some fresh thinking now.

The panic which had taken hold of him since the blowing up of the bank started to subside under the demands of his will. This was still the chance of his lifetime and now was not the moment to lose his nerve. He must harden himself. Vast fortunes were not won by men who were ruled by the gentler emotions. He heard himself say in a cold voice which he scarcely recognised as his own: 'I think it would be better for all of us if this McAllister was killed.'

Stevenson raised an eyebrow in surprise. What Lindholm said made sense, but Stevenson had never expected him to say it.

'You've changed your tune, Lindholm,' he said.

The banker said: 'The game's changed. It changed the moment Barker was killed. It could be any of us next. I know this town. Like all such towns, it'll follow a strong leader, but it'll go to pieces without him. Kill McAllister, and we can finish this job while they're all catching their breath.'

The Kid said: 'This sounds more and more like my kind of business.'

Stevenson said half-mockingly: 'So you're volunteering to knock McAllister over?'

'Sure,' said the Kid, who liked to look tough in front of women. 'You think he can't be killed or something?'

Stevenson said: 'It's been tried a good few times before without any notable success.'

The Kid smiled. 'Maybe his luck just ran out.'

Lindholm nodded. 'That's good, so far as it goes. Now, the gold. If the Kid takes risks and we put ourselves in jeopardy by killing a sheriff, it must be to good purpose. We have to locate Ramage's main source of gold.'

'Put a gun to his head and offer to blow his brains out,' the Kid said. 'It's simple and it works like a charm.'

Stevenson said: 'Ramage knows we can't afford to kill him. Not before we find the gold.'

Lindholm said, liking himself in his new calm and master of destiny part: 'So let's all have a drink and talk about this.'

Stevenson laughed. 'I never heard of a better idea.'

A number of incidents took place during that night and the following day which are pertinent to this story.

First, the Kid.

He knew a thing or two about McAllister. Who did not, in his trade? He knew that the man was tough and capable and incorruptible. But he knew that the strongest factor McAllister had going for him was his luck. And the Kid believed in Luck with a capital L as if she was a goddess. To beat a man's luck when it was strong, you had to have powerful odds on your side. The best odds the Kid could think of was a powerful long-distance rifle, a few shells and surprise. Nothing on earth, except for an act of God, could guard a man against that combination.

So the Kid thought about it. The easiest shot he could get at the sheriff was right here in town. But that was risky. A man could get himself caught too easily in a town. He needed a location where space and distance were his allies. Which meant somewhere near McAllister's ranch. There was good cover on the high ridges above the place, and he could ride hard from there to comparative safety. The ranch was the one place where McAllister would go, sooner or later.

Having made up his mind to this, the Kid eased out of town under cover of dark and took up a position on a ridge between the ranch house and the high ridges on the far side of the road. From his hiding place, he could run with equal ease down the length of the valley to the hills beyond or back on to the wooded ridge, where he would have good cover and could knock over any pursuit. He would have liked a weapon with a longer range than his Spencer carbine, but there was none other then available.

As for the others in the banker's house – they had a problem. The girl, Carla Blount, for whom J. Howard Lindholm had such definite plans, had been in his house a number of days without daring to put her head outside for fear of being seen. So far as the town was concerned, she had disappeared into thin air. There was no future for her shut up in the house, and she was growing increasingly restless and uneasy. She voiced her need to get clear of the town, and Stevenson suggested that if they could get her to Caspar, she could travel on to Chicago without too much trouble. But she was having none of that and bluntly told them so. She had a stake in this enterprise and she did not mean to take her eyes off her colleagues until the gold was in her hands. When Stevenson ventured: 'But you can trust us, Carla,' she laughed, and he did not press the claim.

He said: 'The only alternative for the moment is for you to

come out on the trail with us. And that is not possible. You must see that.'

'I don't see it at all,' she told him. 'I can ride and I'm not soft.'

Lindholm did not like the idea at all. Having got his hands on a beautiful woman, he did not want to risk her in the dangers of the wild. Just the same, he admired Carla for her grit. But he did not like the way in which Stevenson spoke to her. Nor how he looked at her. He had his suspicions that they had known each other before Stevenson had hired her in Chicago to impersonate Allison Disart. He hated the idea of days in the saddle and the rigours of the trail, but his desire for the woman was very great.

'I think I should go along, too,' he said.

Stevenson disagreed almost violently. 'Out of the question, Howard. Your departure'll only arouse suspicion of your complicity in town here.'

'You think they don't smell a rat already? My days here are numbered. I have been thinking about getting out all day. I have the right, Hank. It's my scheme, you might say.'

Stevenson looked at the girl and could almost see her brain making its calculations, weighing the advantages and disadvantages of having Lindholm along. She decided and said: 'Howie certainly has the right. I think he should come.'

Stevenson did not like the tone of equality in the girl's voice. 'Don't get above yourself, Carla,' he said. 'Remember, all I did was hire you to play the girl's part. You didn't have any further share in the plunder. You worked for wages.'

'The contract's null and void,' she pushed back at him quickly. 'You didn't say anything about me being in physical danger. You didn't say anything about me being hidden in this house for days. All I had to do was an acting job and go back home.'

'Nothing's stopping you.'

Lindholm said with his new resolution: 'I'm stopping her, Hank. Carla and I have an understanding.' Stevenson started to look mad, and the banker did not fail to notice it. 'I think we owe her something more than wages and I think my opinion carries some weight still in this enterprise.'

Now the big man showed the extent of his control, that he was a man who could bide his time. 'All right, if that's the way you feel. I've paid off Madders and the other men. They've headed back for the Hole in the Wall country. Now we can all clear out and take Joe Ramage with us. His damned niece too, if we have to. Maybe Joe'll change his mind if he thinks a pretty girl is going to get her throat cut.'

Lindholm looked horrified. 'My God,' he said, 'I'm not going to stand for a woman being killed.'

Stevenson laughed. 'Nobody intends to kill her, Howard. Rest easy.'

But when Lindholm looked at Stevenson, he could not rid himself of the feeling that here was a man who would stop at nothing if the need arose. When he glanced at Carla, he knew the girl thought the same.

Stevenson poured himself another drink and said easily: 'Now, let's decide how we take old Joe. It has to be done tonight. The Kid's off to settle McAllister's hash, so it's up to the three of us.'

Carla smiled and said: 'This is where I earn my new interest in the scheme, Hank. Joe's not going to take alarm when a distressed female walks into his house.'

They both stared at her, and Stevenson laughed again. 'Carla,' he said, 'you're a great girl.'

Lindholm said: 'I hope there's no danger in it for you.'

22

There were times when McAllister was readier to believe his father's tale about the Cheyenne being his mother rather than the high-born Mexican lady. His reasons were good enough. His instincts were Indian. When he heard a warning in his head, he did not argue with it. It had proved itself too right too many times.

It was late and he was walking down Main in the direction of the livery, when suddenly he saw Joe Ramage in his mind's eye so clearly that it startled him. It had been his intention to saddle up and ride to his own place for an hour or two just to see that his stock were all right. Now he stopped, hestitated a moment and, instead of turning left towards the livery barn and corral, kept on down the street to its intersection with Morrow, where he turned right for Joe Ramage's house.

The streets were almost empty. Two men stood in weak lamplight and argued about a hand in the game of poker they had just left. A drunk sang to the moon with the voice of a discordant coyote. McAllister stepped round him. He could see the white picket fence of Joe's house ahead of him at the end of the street.

Halfway down Morrow, it occurred to him that, if his warning instincts were correct, it might be as well to approach Joe's house unseen. He changed direction, walked between two new building plots and out to the backlots. He made his way as quietly as he could through the trash thrown there and so came to the as yet unnamed street which lay parallel to Main. The skeletons of one or two projected houses rose pale and almost ghostly in the moonlight. He passed between them and circled to come at Joe's house from the rear.

Now he moved with enormous caution, for he had no wish for Charlie Stellino to blast a round ball of lead into him. Halting, he listened. He heard nothing expect for the sound of a dog barking tirelessly on the far side of town. He wondered where Charlie was, and guessed that he was most likely on the move to prevent himself falling asleep.

He went forward six silent Indian paces and stopped.

He had heard something.

When he had identified the nature of the sound and its location, he went forward with maybe a little less caution.

Charlie had his back to a tree. His mouth was open and his eyes were closed. He was snoring. McAllister kicked him none too gently and said: 'Wake up, you idle bastard.'

Charlie woke up, scratched himself and said: 'Better men than you've gotten theyselves shot for coming up on me thataway.'

McAllister said softly: 'Charlie, you stay awake or I'll have your guts for galluses, hear?'

'Sure,' said Charlie.

'I'm going to mosey around the back of the house. If you mistake me for a road agent and shoot me, I'm going to be mad at you. If you mistake a road agent for me and let him get away, I'll be mad at you.'

Charlie looked a little surly. 'I can't win.'

'You win if you behave above average for your record, say like a dimwit.'

'You'll insult me once too often.'

'I'll catch you sleeping once too often. Now get on your feet and keep your eyes open.'

Charlie crawled up the tree trunk to his feet and turned to speak to McAllister. He was a little shocked when he failed to find his friend. It gave him the creeps when McAllister acted that way.

'Jesus,' he said to himself, 'it ain't natural.'

McAllister froze about thirty paces from where he had left Charlie. Somebody was approaching the house from the west. He waited no more than a count of five before a slender form came into view. He could not see it clearly, but he realised that this was Allison Disart's impersonator. She crossed from right to left of his vision, opened the gate in the picket fence and started towards the kitchen door.

He heard her tap on the door. No light showed, but he heard the door open. There was a whispered conversation. Then he saw her go inside and the door close behind her.

'The damn fool,' said McAllister.

He turned his ear slowly through one hundred and eighty degrees as he laid his acute hearing across the night. If the girl was here, ten to one, one or two of her colleagues were around.

A night bird cried eerily over the valley, and the sound struck a chill through the listening man. It was as if he had heard the cry of a lost soul in the night.

Softly, there came a sound from near at hand. His right hand slid to the butt of the Remington and he started to ease it from the holster. But the weapon never cleared leather. Something struck him hard at the base of his skull and he felt himself pitching violently forward. He did not fall directly to the ground, for something else struck him another blow from the side. It was as though his head had exploded like a bomb. In the dark, far off, he heard a faint scream, drawn out like a thinly-stretched thread.

It was dawn and he was shaking. He was shaking because he was cold. He groaned when he tried to sit up. His joints were agonisingly stiff. His head thudded and ached beyond endurance.

His first thought was: Why the hell didn't they kill me?

He got to his feet and steadied himself against a tree. A few minutes later, he found Charlie lying on his back with his mouth open and his eyes closed once more. McAllister decided not to kick him awake this time. He dropped to one knee beside Charlie and gently shook him.

'Charlie,' he said softly.

To his amazement, Charlie at once opened his eyes. A look of utter dismay showed on his face when he saw McAllister.

'Hell, Rem,' he said, 'I must of dropped off for a couple of minutes.'

McAllister said: 'It's daylight.'

Charlie sat up and smiled shyly. 'You're right. I'm sorry, Rem – say, what happened to you?'

McAllister said, with an understandable bitterness: 'Somebody tried to break my skull within spitting distance of you, you son-of-a-bitch.'

Charlie swallowed. 'I guess,' he said, 'there ain't too much I can say.'

'No,' said McAllister, 'there ain't. Let's go see if they took the old man.'

Charlie rose, inspected McAllister's head and the congealed blood on it and tut-tutted righteously. They walked together to the house. McAllister was never quite sure how he made it. The world pitched crazily around him and he had a powerful inclination to throw up.

The kitchen door was open and they went inside. Nothing that they could see had been disturbed. They searched the whole house and found no sign of Joe or the girl. McAllister told Charlie: 'Cook some breakfast. Plenty of coffee. We ain't going to find 'em fast and we ain't going to find them any better on empty bellies.'

Charlie said: 'Being up all night always works an appetite for me.'

McAllister said: 'Is that a fact?'

He went through the house again carefully, while Charlie slaved over a hot stove. Over ham and eggs and several cups of coffee well laced with sugar, McAllister still wondered why they had not killed him.

When they were through eating, Charlie said: 'If they have the old man and the girl, there ain't much we can do, Rem. They're hostages like.'

'You're right,' McAllister said.

Charlie went on: 'A posse on their trail will be as good as putting a gun to Joe's and Miss Allison's heads.'

'That's a fact,' McAllister said.

'So what's to do?'

'Wa-al,' said McAllister, 'either one man follows them that knows his business. Or we make a guess at their line of march and get ahead of them.'

Charlie looked as if he believed McAllister was wrong in the head. 'You can't guess where they're headed.'

McAllister said: 'Let's go see Mark.'

They found Tully asleep in his room over the saloon. They would have knocked if they thought he had company. How were they to know he was enjoying bedtime companionship with a handsome Italian girl from the restaurant on Morrow? She was new in town and they had not even gotten around to knowing her name and here was Tully . . . It sure caught a man's breath to contemplate the speed at which a man of Tully's mature years could move.

Tully swore some, but he took it very well, considering. McAllister apologised with his usual courtesy and advised the girl that if she covered her superb upper torso with a bedcover nobody would be shocked, though they might be a little disappointed. She smiled bewitchingly and sank almost out of sight.

Tully said: 'Can't a man get any privacy in this town?'

'Not at times like this,' McAllister informed him.

'What kind of a time is this?' Tully wanted to know.

McAllister told him.

When he was through, Tully swung his legs over the side of the bed. Suddenly he was very much awake. 'Boys,' he said, 'we're in one hell of a fix. We don't have any idea where Joe's gold is. He never came into town twice from the same direction.'

'I've been thinking about that,' McAllister said. 'I reckon this is gambling time. We're not going to get old Joe or the girl back safely without a gamble. I'm betting Joe won't tell these villains where his gold is straight off. He's an obstinate old man. He ain't told a living soul so far where his digging is. He's going to keep his secret to the last minute. He knows damn well I'll follow him and he'll play them along till he can't do it any more. So he takes them in the wrong direction to start off.'

Tully said: 'You could be right. But, by God, you could be wrong. And being wrong could get those two dead.'

Charlie said: 'We don't know they're killers.'

Tully said: 'They ain't ready to kiss us either, that's for sure after what they did to Mose Copley. You seen that Stevenson? There's a cold one if you like.'

'Got a map?' said McAllister.

'Sure, in the office.' He turned to the girl. 'Keep the bed warm, honey. I'll be right back.'

'Not for a few days, you won't,' McAllister said.

Tully rolled his eyes to the ceiling and said: 'Here we go. Best go on home, sweetheart. Tell your old man you worked late.'

'He'll kill me,' the girl said.

Tully told: 'You tell him, if he kills you, I'll kill him.'

She said: 'If he thought we were to be married, he would be nice about it.'

Tully walked out of the room, hauling his pants after him

and saying: 'I didn't hear that. Neither did you fellers.'

Going downstairs, McAllister said: 'You could do worse, Mark. At your age.'

'Hear, hear,' said Charlie.

Tully shuddered. He poured them each a whiskey in his office. Nobody cared how early it was. There was a hard trail ahead of them and no drink. Tully found the map and found the Breaks at the far end of the valley, to the northwest.

'I reckon old Joe'll lead 'em into the Breaks and then into the Blue Feather area. There's always been talk of gold there. It would sound reasonable to them.'

Tully opined that it could be. But he had his doubts. Charlie did not have an idea on the subject. His thoughts were that they would have to run the villains down. It would end by Joe and the girl getting hurt and everybody making smoke.

'There's a hang-rope at the end of this,' he said, 'you mark my words.' He sounded distressed. He did not like violence. He always got hurt.

McAllister said: 'Mark, you get three or four good men together, go to the top of the valley and head on straight into the hills and work your way around to Blue Rock. I'll try and meet you there in two days. Maybe you can head them off before they reach Blue Feather. Grub for a week.'

Tully said: 'All right.' He never fussed when he knew what there was to do. 'What about you?'

'I'll pick up their tracks and follow them.'

'What if they see you?' Charlie said.

Tully said confidently: 'They won't see him. What about Charlie, Rem?'

McAllister said: 'Best take him along with you. And see he don't shoot himself.'

He walked out to the street through the saloon. There were two men sleeping on the floor and one drinking sadly and steadily at the bar. McAllister walked up Main to the livery and found Lon McKenna watering the horses. McAllister told Lon he would be wanted for a posse, and the mayor said: 'My wife ain't going to believe this.' McAllister saddled, mounted and rode for home.

Lige was forking hay in the barn when he rode in. He had saddled the powerful gelding canelo, Oscar, and led him out into the yard when Mose Copley walked across the little bridge over the creek from his own house. He walked slowly and he limped. His head was still bandaged. McAllister did not think that he should be up and walking, but he knew it would be no good to say so.

McAllister said: 'They've taken Joe Ramage and the girl.'

Mose nodded and said: 'What about that bank man, Lindholm?'

McAllister had not given him a thought. Now he did, and he reckoned it did not make any difference to anything what Lindholm did. The situation could not be worse.

He said: 'I'll be gone a week maybe,' and Mose said: 'Right, boss.' McAllister filled his saddle pockets with food from the kitchen, most of it jerky and beans. He packed powder, shot, caps and bullet mould. Just in case. He did not forget his horse. Maybe there would be time to stop for grass, maybe not. He tied a gunnysack of corn to the saddle-horn.

Mose and Luge watched him mount and ride out. Mose said: 'You watch out for yourself, man.' Bella did not show herself. McAllister headed straight past the house, intending to go directly north along the valley.

He had covered no more than fifty yards before something hit the bow of his saddle a hard blow, catching the gelding in mid-stride and making him stagger. Then came the flat, distant slam of a rifle.

McAllister did not hesitate, but brought his quirt down sharply on Oscar's rump. The powerful horse stretched himself out into a hard run. The rifle sounded again before they bolted into cover of the string of thickets which stretched across the valley. McAllister halted the horse and it stood blowing lustily. Back at the house, Mose was yelling something. There was a pause and he heard Bella's piercing commands. He could guess what was happening. And a few moments later, he knew he was right. Mose and his son came riding hard from behind the barn, heading up the ridge towards the trees. McAllister at once touched the gelding with the quirt and drove him forward. He heaved the Henry from the saddle boot and burst through the thickets into the open.

Suddenly, the open space between himself and the trees at the top of the ridge before him seemed interminable. There was no sound but that of Oscar's hoofs and the creak of saddle-leather. He glanced left and saw that Mose and Lige were coming on hard, their horses breasting the start of the slope. Both men were armed. Turning his attention back to the trees above him, he saw a small scurry of movement. The marksman had taken alarm.

He thought he heard the sound of another shot. Alarmed, he looked at Mose and his son and saw to his relief that both were still in the saddle. Part of McAllister's brain told him that he should approach the timber with caution, but the reckless habits of a lifetime were too much for him. Anger ruled where cool thought should have guided him. However, the luck which perhaps he did not deserve saved him and, as he burst into the trees, his eyes darting everywhere in search of movement, he saw the sunlight hit the thin line of a rifle barrel. He swung Oscar right towards it, circling a tree and pounding on west. Within seconds, he could see the open grassland beyond the trees and there, no more than a hundred yards ahead of him, was a racing horse with a man crouched over its extended neck. He drew rein and dropped from the saddle, telling Oscar to stand, in a voice which the animal obeyed instantly.

He laid the barrel of the Henry across the saddle and heard the other two riders crashing through the trees behind him. Even as he fired, he knew he'd made a hit. The shot laid the man flat along the horse's neck. McAllister waited, expecting the motion of the horse to shake the wounded man from the saddle, but this did not happen. He levered another round into the breech, but the horse and rider were gone before he could fire, dipping down into a fold in the land.

He swore, and Mose Copley went past him yelling like an Indian.

At the top of his voice, McAllister bellowed: 'Mose, you come back here.' Bella was uppermost in his mind.

Lige went past on the run, all Comanche and yelling for blood.

McAllister roared: 'Lige, you hold up or you're fired.'

He might as well have been shouting at the wind.

'Goddammit to hell,' he said, and vaulted back into the saddle. Oscar was running before his feet were in the irons. 'I'll skin those two bastards alive when I catch up with them.'

He caught sight of the marksman heaving up a farther ridge. His three pursuers were all well mounted. McAllister could only assume that the quarry's horse was superb. It stretched away north as if the slope of the ridge gave it no problem at all. The pace was a terrible one and no horse could be expected to keep it up for long except on the flat, and McAllister did not fancy having three of his best horses ruined in pursuit of a wounded man. Besides that, he had other ideas about the purpose the wounded man could serve. McAllister wanted the kidnappers, and this man, if luck did its job, would lead him to them.

He used his quirt again and Oscar, who was not used to the whip and did not like it, hit a pace that was equal to any horse's on earth. He showed his quality now, no doubt urged on by McAllister's furious bellows for his two crew members to draw rein. At last, not even they could ignore the commands of their boss and came sulkily to a halt.

Mose was fit to be tied. His ugly face was all screwed up with rage.

'You know what you just did?' he demanded, getting the words out with the greatest difficulty. 'You robbed me of my just rights. You wasn't beat to no pulp. I owed one of them bastards. I wanted to get my hands around that trash's throat and squeeze the goddam life out of him.'

Lige was a little milder, but he was not looking kindly on McAllister.

'Boss, you shouldn't ought to of did that. That son-of-a-bitch's hide belongs to my old man, and you know it.'

'All right, all right,' McAllister snarled. 'I get your drift, but all this ain't been set up for your satisfaction. I want the feller to lead me to the rest. Besides, I can't face up to Bella again if one of you two get's lead in his fool hide. She won't kill you, you're family.'

Mose cracked his face in a wide grin. 'Wa-al,' he said, 'may be the son-of-a-bitch'll bleed to death. Just you keep him moving, boss, so he can't tie hisself up.'

'That's a promise,' McAllister said. 'Now you high-tail it back to the house and prove beyond all possible doubt to Bella you ain't even scratched.'

They looked like they were going to argue, but McAllister rode away from them shouting: 'See you,' and sent Oscar up-valley at an easy canter.

'Maybe I should trail him, pa,' Lige said. 'You could tell ma I went into town or something.'

Mose was tempted, but he shook his head. 'Home, son.'

'Aw, pa.'

'Home.'

23

Offdike was a tall, lean man with a cold brain. Nominally he was subordinate to Stevenson, but in fact Offdike was subordinate to nobody and never had been, not in all his life since the age of thirteen when, man-size, he had stuck three inches of jack-knife blade into the man who had taken him from an orphanage and called himself his guardian. That had been in Illinois twenty years before. Offdike had headed West then, and he had stayed West. There was still room here for a man with initiative. And initiative to Offdike meant taking what you wanted, when you wanted it. Unless the man who held that something was stronger than you were. In which case you walked around him.

It was Offdike who had organised the trip – horses, mules, supplies, everything. And it would quite likely be Offdike who got the truth out of old Joe Ramage. Stevenson appeared to trust him, and J. Howard Lindholm could not see why. Stevenson seemed a worldly enough fellow and should have known better. The banker did not like Offdike and he did not trust him. Cold though he might be, the way he looked at Carla was far from cold. More than once during that terrible ride, Lindholm told himself that if they ever found the gold, he would not put it past Offdike to attempt to get away with the treasure and the girl.

Admittedly, Lindholm's temper was tried to its limit by the incessant riding. He could ride well enough, but his backside was not made to be in a saddle for twelve hours at a stretch.

'We have to get to the gold and clear it out before any kind of pursuit gets close,' Stevenson had said. 'Then we each take our share and we scatter. Several trails are harder to follow than one.'

That first night in camp, several miles beyond the Black Horse Breaks, Lindholm said: 'The gold you took from the coach, Hank. Now we're nearing the end of the trail, I think we should all know where you cached it.'

That seemed to take the big man back a bit. 'All in good time, Howard,' he said. 'It's safe enough, never fear.'

The others were all listening, and Lindholm decided not to press the matter in front of them. He would get the truth out of Stevenson when they were alone. It was his right to know. After all, he was the originator of this whole scheme. If it had not been for him . . .

He looked round at the others. Carla, bearing up wonderfully well under the physical strain of all the hard riding. He tried to catch her eye and failed. He had failed to do that a good deal in the last twenty-four hours, and that worried him. He blamed it on Stevenson, who had been remorselessly charming to the girl ever since they had slipped out of town with their two prisoners.

He heard Offdike's softly rasping voice – 'It ain't the gold you should be fretting about, Mr Lindholm. It's the Kid.'

A small flutter of unease went through Lindholm. 'The Kid?'

Stevenson said: 'Why isn't he here?'

'It's a long ride,' the banker said.

Offdike said: 'He should of caught us long since.' He laughed, and the sound was like the short, sharp bark of a kid fox. 'Maybe that McAllister don't knock over so easy.'

The full import of this came ramming home to Lindholm. He knew about McAllister better than anybody here. He was an Indian if ever there was one. A savage. He felt panic clutch at his throat like a strangling hand.

'What can we do?' he said. Stevenson and Offdike were looking at him sardonically. He knew they both despised him.

'Two things,' Stevenson said immediately. 'One, we make the old man talk because we don't have any time now to fool around. Two, we kill McAllister.'

'Supposing he has a whole posse with him? There's some mighty able men in Black Horse.'

Stevenson smiled and showed the gold in his teeth. 'No, McAllister won't hang around for a posse. If the Kid missed him, he'll come fast and alone. I know about McAllister.'

They all turned their heads to look at Joe Ramage, who lay bound hand and foot on the edge of the circle of light from the fire. The girl Allison crouched beside him. She had to crouch, because her hands were tied to her ankles. She looked sick and scared.

Carla said: 'The girl's the answer. Slip a little steel into Ally and the old man'll crack.' She smiled tight-lipped at her former room-mate. Allison's eyes were huge and terrified in her pinched face. None of the men could believe that she had been beautiful so short a time before.

Stevenson rose to his feet and walked over to them. He kicked Joe lightly in the ribs and said: 'Think about it through the night, old man. We'll start carving the girl in the morning. Just lie there and think about it. You tell us where the gold is, and we won't have any reason to hurt either of you. We are not killers, Joe. Tell us where the gold is, and we'll leave you with a couple of horses. I can't say fairer than that.'

The old man did not utter a word. His eyes snapped with rage and hatred.

The girl Allison said: 'I can't believe this is happening. Carla, how can you let them do this?'

'I can't stop them,' Carla said. 'Even if I wanted.'

Stevenson kicked Joe Ramage again. Quite gently.

'Get thinking, old man,' he said. 'It's the knife for the girl if you don't.'

Joe's voice came now in a high-pitched, keening whine – 'You bastards. You low-down yeller bastards.'

Offdike said: 'I suggest we kill the fire and move camp before we hit the sack. No telling who's sighted us here.'

'Good idea,' said Stevenson.

The Kid was scared. He was sick with fear. He was scared because he was wounded and bleeding. He was scared in case he was being followed and his pursuers might catch him. He was scared because he might be leading his pursuers to the rest of the gang. He knew Offdike and Stevenson. They were like him. A human life meant no more to them than that of a coyote. If they thought he had betrayed them, they would kill him.

He cursed himself for attempting a shot that was at too long a range for his carbine. He had overestimated himself and the weapon. His mistake was unforgivable. It was the kind of thing a greenhorn would do. The man who had shot him had made no such error. The bullet had hit him high in the right shoulder. He reckoned his shoulder blade was shattered, but, strange though it seemed, the wound had hurt very little in the first minutes. Now, as he reached the northern end of the valley, the full effect of the injury hit him. He felt the pain and the shock of it. The pain sickened him; the shock had him trembling in the saddle like a girl. At first he seemed to burn up, then suddenly he was cold and he thought he would die of cold.

He knew that he was bleeding and he wanted to stop and staunch the blood, but he dared not while there was a chance that there was a pursuer close behind him. Once or twice, he turned painfully in the saddle to take a look at his back trail, but he failed to find even a single rider there. There should have been at least three – McAllister, who had charged him, and the two black riders who had been yelling like Indians. But now the valley showed no movement except for that of cattle and a small bunch of range horses.

Turning into the Breaks, he began to cheer up a little. It looked safe enough for him to stop and try to do something about his wound. He waited until he came to water. This came in the form of a narrow trickle in the bottom of a gully. It was not too sweet, but it was water, and he dismounted to drink copiously. He thought he would never be able to satisfy his giant thirst. When his stomach was distended with water, he stopped himself and tried to get off his coat and shirt. This hurt him a lot and he had to drive himself on to do it. Finally, the upper part of his body was bare, and he used his bandanna to wash the wound as best he could. The cold of the water made him feel a little better, but the pain was very great now and the intensity of it was scary.

The Kid might be any number of low things, but he was tough and he had grit. He made up his mind that he was not going to bleed to death. He was going to reach the others and he was going to have his share of that gold. He fixed his mind on the gold. If he kept thinking about the gold he would get through this all right.

Through a great wall of pain, he tied the wet bandanna over his right shoulder. It would not have been easy to do unhurt; hurt as he was, he went through the tortures of the damned. To keep the crude bandage in place, he tied a strip of rawhide to the front of the bandage, passed the thong around his body and managed with great difficulty to secure it to the bandage behind him. With that done, he felt as though he had gained a major victory and his spirits rose. He was weak from loss of blood, but he drank some more water and thought maybe that would help. He threw the bloody shirt away and found a fresh one in a saddle pocket. He managed to get into it, but found that his coat pained his wound too much, so he tied it behind his saddle.

Then he was in the saddle and heading down the Breaks. He was still thinking about the gold.

McAllister watched the boy from the rim of the Breaks. When he saw him ride off due west, going slowly, he was pleased, because it looked as if he was heading where McAllister wanted him to go. This way, McAllister might find himself in the vicinity of Blue Rock when the posse turned up there.

The Kid was still in the Breaks when night came down. The boy halted and made camp in the rocks below. McAllister off-saddled and catnapped where he was, knowing that the sound of the Kid moving in the morning would reach him at his height. When the Kid moved, he would move. Maybe would lead him to Joe and the girl.

The following morning, while mist shrouded the lower reaches of the Breaks, McAllister watched the ghostly figure of the boy below through his glass. The Kid's movements were slow and painful. McAllister watched his agonised efforts to saddle and mount his horse and could not help wondering if the boy would be able to reach his friends. When at last the boy was in the saddle, even at that distance McAllister could see that the effort to stay in the saddle was almost too much for him. McAllister decided that he would not last the day out.

No sooner did he decide this, than he decided on the action he should take. This was no time to be delaying. He had to reach Joe and the girl as quickly as he could. One way, of course, would be to get ahead of the Kid and pick up Stevenson's tracks. But he doubted that the prisoners had been brought this way. They would have been taken across country through the hills to some point northwest of here. So he lifted his lines and urged Oscar to a brisker pace, descended to lower country a couple of miles further on and worked his way through the broken land at the west of the Breaks where he might expect to intercept the Kid.

24

None of the men liked it – except maybe Offdike, but his face did not admit or deny his liking for dealing out pain to a woman. Stevenson for one would not have hesitated to put any man to the torture if his compensation was high enough. But all his instincts went against dealing out pain to a woman. He liked women too much. So, when it came to it, he started sweating. And Offdike's mocking gaze on him when he stood over Allison Disart with his knife blade bared did not help. He would have offered the weapon to Offdike, but he feared the atrocity the man might commit.

They had all been awake an hour now. Breakfast had been hastily eaten without enjoyment. Everybody's nerves were bare this morning.

Stevenson bent over Ramage and said: 'What kind of a mean-hearted bastard are you, Joe, that you could see a woman hurt?'

Joe spat back: 'You harm that girl, Stevenson, and there won't be a man in this country won't fight to get a strangle-rope around your neck.'

Which was true enough. That did not faze Stevenson. A good many men wanted him dead, in any case.

Stevenson took hold of Joe by his scant hair and heaved his head off the ground. 'Joe, we can't kill you, because we want you to show us where the gold is. But we can kill the girl. You want to have her on your conscience for the rest of your life. You'll think of her every time you think of the gold.'

From where he sat sombre and grey on his rock, Offdike said: 'I can kill the girl,' and the words hung on the air, like an unmentionable threat.

Stevenson stood up abruptly. 'All right,' he said, 'kill the girl. Get it over with. I've lost patience with this old fool.'

Offdike stood up and drew his sheath knife. 'Where do I do it?' he said calmly.

Stevenson glanced at Carla and saw that she was sitting stiff with horror. He shifted his gaze quickly from her and said: 'Here. Right here, so Joe can see the result of his obstinacy.'

Offdike said in that softly grating voice of his: 'I aim to mark her some with the point, just to see how Joe takes that. If he don't talk then, I'll cut her throat.'

Carla said in a breathless explosion of words: 'No. You can't do it.'

Lindholm was alarmed to hear himself say: 'Carla's right. Threatening the old man turns my stomach. Harming the girl is not to be contemplated. With my stake in this affair, I should say that my opinion is authoritative.'

Stevenson and Offdike were staring at him. He did not care. A rogue he might be, but he was no barbarian. Besides which, if they harmed the girl, retribution against them could be terrible.

Stevenson said: 'If you two don't want the gold, why, you get on your horses and ride. You're welcome.'

'Our deal did not take in murder or torture.'

Stevenson said: 'It does now.'

Allison Disart said: 'Uncle Joe, for God's sake tell them. Do you value your gold above me?'

'That ain't fair,' Joe yelped. 'My God, how that ain't fair. I worked all my life to find this kind of claim. Now I got it, it's took away from me.'

Offdike walked across to Allison and, taking her chin in his left hand, raised her head so that she was forced to look up at him.

'You just take a look at me, girl,' he said. 'I bet the touch and feel of me makes your blood run cold.'

True, the girl was shuddering uncontrollably.

'Jesus,' said old Joe, 'this ain't fair.'

Offdike pricked the pale forehead with the sharp point of his knife. Joe saw the small spurt of blood. He started to struggle frantically against his rawhide bonds, but they would have held a man twice his strength.

Stevenson watched him and laughed. 'All you have to do, Joe,' he said, 'is tell us where the gold is.'

Joe stopped struggling. 'I'll do a deal,' he said.

Lindholm had never experienced such relief in his whole life. He swore angrily when Stevenson said: 'No deals. Just tell us where the gold is.'

Lindholm said: 'Maybe you don't care for deals. But I do, Hank. I'll do any kind of deal that gets us gold.'

Stevenson glowered at him for a moment, then said: 'Let's hear it.'

Joe said: 'I got a whole lot of gold cached at the diggings. You keep the girl while I go get you some more gold. My God, there's enough there for a hundred men.'

Before Lindholm could say anything, Stevenson said: 'No deal. You're so gold-crazy, you'd take off and leave us with the girl.'

'What guarantee do I have,' Joe said, 'that you won't kill us both after you gets your hands on the gold.'

Offdike laughed and said: 'You don't.'

Lindholm said sharply: 'Offdike, I'd be obliged if you'd remember that you are one partner in a partnership of five. Joe, you have my guarantee. Lead us to the gold. We'll hold you while we get the gold out, then we'll set you free.'

'Sure,' said Stevenson. 'You may not trust me and Offdike, but you've got to trust Lindholm and Carla. They're soft.'

Joe lay there squirming, unable to commit himself totally. But at last he said: 'All right. I'll do it. Get these goddam rawhides off'n me and I'll do it. But you keep away from the girl or the deal's off. Hear?'

Stevenson looked mockingly at Lindholm and then at Carla. 'How about it,' he said, 'you agree?'

Carla said: 'I agree. We get the gold, then we set the two of them free. The only thing we'll gain if we kill them will be the hatred of everybody in these parts.'

'I concur with that entirely,' Lindholm said.

'All right,' Stevenson said. 'Let's saddle up and ride. But, Joe you get tricky with us and I'll forget all about the girl and maybe the gold too, because I'll break your back.'

He and Offdike went off to fetch the horses. Lindholm turned to Carla and said gratefully: 'You were wonderful, my dear, and I shan't forget it.'

Allison Disart said: 'We thank you too, Carla.'

Carla said: 'I'm soft when it comes to killing you in cold blood, Ally. But you won't find me soft when it comes to getting the gold. You and the old man best not try fooling around.'

When they were saddled and ready, Stevenson said: 'The Kid's on my mind. Something's got to have happened to him. One of us should go back and check.'

Offdike said: 'That sounds like my line of work. If the little bastard's leading them town boys to us, I'll settle his hash, and theirs too.'

'All right,' Stevenson told him, 'go ahead.' He turned to Joe Ramage and demanded: 'What direction you leading us in, Joe?'

The old man hesitated. Then he said: 'The gold's not far from a place called the Eagle's Nest. That's a cave about one mile west of Blue Rock. Know it?'

Offdike said: 'I know it.' He lifted his lines and moved his horse away.

When Lindholm was in the saddle, he said: 'You are trying my trust too far, Hank, by not telling either Carla or me where the stage gold is hidden.'

Stevenson smiled disarmingly. 'Hell,' he said, 'it isn't any great secret, man. It's kind of laughable really. It's cached in a small side cave off the Eagle's Nest. Seemed the right place. Me and Offdike have used the place as a hideout so many times.'

Joe Ramage said: 'This has to be one of life's little jokes, me digging out my gold, toting it into town and you bringing it back up here again.'

Stevenson swung around in the saddle and said through

his teeth in sudden and unexpected rage: 'By Christ, Ramage, you'd best not be playing another of life's little jokes.'

25

McAllister stayed up on high ground until about four hours after dawn. Until then, the boy he was following had made slow progress and seemed reluctant to put his horse at any pace faster than a quick walk. Even then, the animal would occasionally stop, as if it were no longer under the control of its rider. It would wander from the trail and drift over to the dried and meagre grass which grew at its side in coarse clumps. Each time, the Kid would apparently rouse himself and guide the animal back on to the trail again. This happened a number of times until the boy pitched from the saddle and lay still. The horse jumped as it felt the weight of the rider go from its back, then once more went to grass and started grazing.

McAllister turned his horse downhill.

The Kid had by now left the Breaks themselves and was working his way along a wide gully into broken country which was a prelude to the foothills. McAllister hit what was little more than a goat track and within a matter of minutes reined in beside the unconscious Kid.

The boy lay face downward with his head twisted to one side. Seeing the bunching of the bandage on the right shoulder, McAllister guessed the position of the wound. He rolled the Kid half over and propped him in a sitting position, holding him in the crook of his left arm and forcing water down his throat from his canteen. The boy choked and opened his eyes. They focused slowly and he said: 'McAllister,' when he recognised the man who held him.

Very softly and very bitterly, he whispered: 'You're too damn late, McAllister. I'm at the end of my rope.'

McAllister smiled rather unpleasantly. 'You're too young and too guilty to die, Kid. Let's get this shirt off you and we'll take a look at the wound.'

When he saw the wound, McAllister did not think it looked too bad, though it did not look too good either.

'Well,' he said, 'you ain't dead yet. I could fix it up for you if we do a deal.'

The Kid looked anxious. 'Is it turning bad?'

'Only a little,' McAllister told him.

'You lying to me?'

'You'll never know,' said McAllister, 'till it's too late.'

The Kid sat there, looking pale as death and thinking. McAllister thought he looked like a pretty well chewed up rat of a fellow. He was not yet twenty, if reports of him were correct, and already he was looking like a wizened old man. His eyes were pure evil. Finally, he said: 'What kind of a deal?'

'The simplest of all. I fix your wound and let you ride off. Just so long as you do ride off. If you don't, I'll kill you.'

'What do I have to do?'

'Tell me where Stevenson is headed.'

'Maybe I don't know.'

'I've been watching you. You haven't been trailing anybody. You know where you're going.'

'I could lie to you.'

'Sure, you could. But you're not going anywhere too fast, Kid. I could ride you down wherever you are.'

The Kid chewed on that awhile. There was something to chew on, too, because if he rode off now he would be saying no to an awful lot of gold. However, gold was no use to a dead man. And he had heard about McAllister. The man was all Indian.

Finally, the Kid said: 'All right. It's a deal. They're waiting for me not too far from Blue Rock.'

McAllister said: 'I'll fix that shoulder for you.'

A voice said: 'You're not fixing anything, McAllister.'

McAllister froze. He knew the voice and he knew there was a gun pointing at his back. The man was in the cover of rocks about thirty paces to his rear. He stood about as much chance as a snowball in hell. So he waited. He looked at the Kid, who had raised himself on one elbow. The Kid and McAllister shared one thought at least – had Offdike heard the Kid tell McAllister where he was headed?

'Reach,' Offdike said, and McAllister raised his hands to shoulder height. 'Higher. Strain yourself, man.' McAllister straightened his arms. He heard the man pacing slowly towards him. He heard the quick intake of breath that always comes immediately before a man strikes a blow. He tried to duck away from it, but he was too late. Something hard caught him below the rim of his hat and he pitched forward over the Kid. The boy tried to throw him off, but he did not possess sufficient strength. McAllister rolled clear and looked up at the tall figure of the man between himself and the sunlight. The brightness was too intense for him to make out any of the details. His senses were reeling from the blow on the head.

Offdike held a repeating carbine, McAllister could make out that much.

'Take that gun from its holster with your left hand, McAllister,' Offdike said. 'Then toss it.'

McAllister obeyed. He hated to treat a good gun that way. Offdike turned his attention to the Kid.

'So you couldn't even kill a man from cover, Kid,' he said conversationally. 'Christ, you're not even any damn use to yourself. Well, you made a deal with McAllister, and you just dealed yourself a place in hell.'

There was no pause, no hesitation. He shot the Kid through the heart. The act was so abrupt and so without warning that McAllister, experienced as he was in the ways of violence and death, was shocked to stillness. It took him a few seconds to collect himself. Offdike moved so that his features cleared. McAllister could see the expression on his face. It was untroubled. He would have shown no more compunction if he had shot an injured horse.

McAllister wanted to know if he had anything to lose by resistance. If he had to die anyway, there was no point in not risking everything in an attempt to get away from Offdike.

He stood up slowly and his head ached abominably. He had been hit on the head once too often recently.

'If you can kill one of your own as easy as that,' he said, 'I don't suppose you'll hesitate to knock me off.'

Offdike said lightly: 'You're right. I wouldn't hesitate. But for the moment, I can use you alive.' He walked over to McAllister's gun and picked it up. He tucked it in the front of his pants. Then he walked to McAllister's horse and pulled the Henry from its scabbard. Then he said: 'Old Joe's reluctant to tell us where his gold mine is. He has tried to mislead us with a lie. When he sees I have you, he will know he's not going to be rescued. Besides, you are a man of common sense, McAllister. You know the kind I am and that I'll stop at nothing. If you convince him that he should tell me the truth for his and the girl's sake, I'll let them both go free.'

McAllister smiled. 'But you won't do the same for me.'

Offdike grinned.

'You're a totally different proposition, Rem.'

They found the others camped about one mile west of Blue Rock. They were now in the wildest country. Not even the small hill ranchers had been bold enough to push their tiny herds this far west. It was a tangle of ravines, scrub, brush and rocks. Water was plentiful. At every turn they seemed to come on long-falling mountain streams and torrents. And it was beautiful. Now the giants of the mountains seemed to hang over them, stooping with their mighty shoulders against the hard blue arc of the sky.

They came on the others near dark, suddenly, tucked away in a ravine that looked as though it had never been trodden by the foot of man.

Lindholm and Carla were on their feet at once. Dismay showed on the faces of the old man and the girl sitting stiffly in their bonds.

Offdike dismounted wearily. Stevenson, puffing a cigar

leisurely at the fire said: 'What happened to the Kid?'
Offdike said: 'He's dead.'
'How?'
'I killed him.'
'Why the hell did you do that?'
'He needed it.' He turned to McAllister and said: 'Get down.' McAllister's hands were tied behind his back. He threw one leg over the saddle-horn, kicked his foot from the stirrup-iron and dropped to the ground.
Joe was so indignant at the sight of him that he found it hard to speak. But he did, just the same. 'My God, McAllister, you was took like a goddam pilgrim.'
McAllister nodded. 'Can't deny it, Joe.' He walked over to the prisoners and sat himself between them. The old man eyed him venomously. Offdike unsaddled the horses and slapped them to join the others on grass nearby. The grass was sparse and scattered. They had to stay free so they could search for feed. The road agents had no hobbles with them. McAllister sat there, taking in all the small facts of that camp. He knew that at most he was within a day of death. He looked at Allison. Now that he was close, he could see that she had sunk into a misery of fear. Joe Ramage was grey-faced, but he was not quite beaten. He had been faced by adversity through too many years for that.
McAllister said softly to the girl: 'Miss Allison, don't you fret now. We'll have you out of this in no time at all.'
Stevenson, seating himself on the ground on the other side of the fire, heard this.
'You're a damn liar,' he said. 'And you know it. The old man lied to us. There's no gold of his near here.'
'There is too,' said Ramage indignantly. 'You think I'd lie with the girl at stake?'
Stevenson said: 'I think you'd lie if your mother was at stake.'
J. Howard Lindholm said earnestly: 'I do implore you, Joe, to tell the truth. I really cannot stomach any more unpleasantness.'
Carla said: 'McAllister, make him see sense. Mr Lindholm and I won't let any harm come to Joe or Allison if he tells the

truth. I swear.'

McAllister said: 'I reckon that doesn't count for too much, honey. I mean, you ain't shown yourself exactly trustworthy this far.'

'I'm sincere when I say I don't want Ally hurt, believe me.'

McAllister turned to the old man: 'Was I you, Joe, I'd reckon we were at the point when the fooling around has to stop. These boys mean business.'

'Rem,' said the old man, 'I reckon with you caught, things don't look too good for me. So, all right. This time it's the truth. I'll kiss a fortune goodbye.'

Offdike strode up to the fire and heard this. 'How far off?' he demanded.

The old man cocked his head on one side and said: 'Couple of hours. No more'n that. Afoot.'

'Hard going?'

'I' ve led burros in and out. You could maybe lead horses.'

Stevenson said: 'We start at daybreak. And this best be the real thing, Joe.'

'It has to be the real thing. It don't give me much of a chance. But it's the only one I have.'

McAllister gave a genuine sigh of relief. The old man had shown sense so much quicker than he had thought possible. Or had he? Was he still lying?

Offdike said: 'We'll split the night into three guards. I'll take the first. You second, Hank. Then Howie.'

Lindholm took exception to the 'Howie'. He said: 'I shall not insist on being Mister Lindholm among colleagues and friends. But "Howie" is pushing it a little too far.'

Offdike chuckled.

McAllister said: 'How about some blankets? There's one behind my saddle.'

Offdike said: 'I hope you get your balls froze off, lawman.'

26

By dawn, McAllister, hard though he was, was stiff with cold. Joe and the girl had rolled close to him to gain and offer warmth. McAllister found the girl a more satisfactory bed-companion than old Joe. During the night, he woke and kissed her on the neck under the ear and she wiggled. He liked that. Hell, he thought, if he was going to die he might as well have a pleasant thought to go out on. He even went so far as to whisper a few encouraging words into her ear. She liked that. Maybe she felt the same as McAllister, because she lifted her mouth to his and kissed him full on the lips. He had never kissed a finer mouth. When Stevenson came close and inspected them, McAllister and the girl were lying back-to-back.

On the far side of the fire, the banker and Carla were sharing their blankets with their arms around each other. The big man smiled to himself. Let them make the most of it – they would not have the opportunity much longer.

Dawn found them hastily finishing their breakfast. They did not feed their prisoners, saying that they would be fed when Joe had led them to the gold. They were surprised when McAllister offered no protest. Offdike and Stevenson brought in the horses and saddled them while Lindholm and the girl packed their gear and supplies. There was an extra horse now the Kid was dead, and they packed what they could on its saddle to save their own horses. They fed Oscar's corn to their own mounts.

They had ridden for no longer than ten minutes when Joe said that they should walk from here on. Stevenson now organised his order of march. Joe Ramage go first, with Stevenson immediately behind him. Then would come Lindholm and Carla, leading the horses. Behind them, walked McAllister and Allison Disart. Leading his own horse and bringing up the rear was Offdike.

They were high now and the early sun was failing to warm this upland world. McAllister began to wonder, as he stumbled through the rocks and brush, that there was gold so high. Maybe this thought was just his ignorance. He had never fancied gold-hunting and knew little more than he had heard from prospectors in saloon talk. They were climbing steadily all the time and the wind was finding them wherever they went, sighing and singing through the rocks. Clouds drifted so close above their heads, it seemed that they could reach out their hands to touch them. Allison's teeth were chattering.

Finally, they found their way on to a small plateau, and suddenly they could see a vast country spread out all around them. In spite of the situation in which he found himself, McAllister stood for a moment, awed by the sight. Allison expressed what was in his mind: 'McAllister, you can't believe there's such things as thieving and murder when you see country like this.'

Offdike hit him between the shoulder blades with the butt of his carbine and drove him on. There followed now a curious sequence of events which stretched McAllister's credulity to its limits.

When they had reached the far side of the plateau, Joe halted and seemed to look around as if he was searching for a way down. Stevenson could not miss the hesitation.

'Old man,' he shouted, 'you lied. You ain't never been here before.'

Joe jumped with fright, but he stood his ground. 'I been here. I know this country like the back of my hand. I'll show you. I ain't never took horses down here before. I was looking for a place where they can find a footing. Even a son-of-a-bitch like you don't want to see a horse break a neck. Even if you do shoot 'em when they pull stages.'

Stevenson would have struck him, but the old man, in

spite of age and his hands being tied behind his back, jumped nimbly out of the way and over the edge of the plateau. There was a great cloud of dust and McAllister knew he'd struck shale. When he reached the edge, he could see the old man rolling and sliding down the slope. Stevenson was forced to go after him. He also lost his footing and went down with a great yell of protest. McAllister would have followed to make the most of the situation, but Offdike was behind him and rammed the muzzle of the repeater into his back, saying: 'Stay still.'

They all somehow negotiated the slope, though Lindholm had the greatest difficulty with the horses and had to be helped by Carla and Stevenson. Nothing would take Offdike from his position at the rear. They came now to an old Indian trail. Old Joe led the way along this at a brisk pace, as if he wanted to rid himself of his gold and get the whole business over and done with. They came down in scrub timber, and this helped to break the wind. For the first time that day, Allison's teeth stopped chattering. McAllister gave her a smile and she managed a smile back. Her nerves were strung tight, as he could see, but she wasn't in the blue scare she'd been in last night. Which was better. There was one right moment ahead of them and McAllister had to recognise it when it came. It might be in a minute or an hour's time. He might be offered no more than a small part of a second by a reckless fate. However small, he had to recognise it and act. He had the lives of the old man and the girl in his hands. Not to mention the fact that his own life was also in the balance. A matter of no small consideration to him.

But you can always rely on life to offer you the unexpected.

Suddenly, Stevenson stopped in his tracks. Lindholm, following behind with the horses, ran into him.

Joe did not halt, but trotted on. He stopped quickly enough when the big man, suddenly into one of his unaccountable furies, bellowed: 'You pull up, old man, or by Christ I'll blow the top of your head off.'

Joe halted as if he had run into a stone wall. He turned and faced Stevenson, his eyes suddenly terrified.

Stevenson walked up to him and caught him by the front of his coat. He jerked at him so that the old man stood on tip-toe.

'You old bastard,' Stevenson yelled into his face, 'you lying old bastard. You think I don't know where I'm at?'

Joe gobbled a bit. Finally, McAllister made out that he said: 'How the hell do I know if you know where you're at?'

Stevenson hurled the thin old body away from him. Joe took three whirling tripping steps like a drunken dancer and fell down.

McAllister started forward, but behind him Offdike said: 'Another step, McAllister, and you're dead. I reckon we don't need you any more, anyway.'

McAllister halted. He said: 'What the hell goes on here?'

Offdike said: 'How should I know? Hank, what goes?'

Stevenson looked blind with rage. His face was almost unrecognisable when he turned it to them. Hoarsely, he shouted: 'Don't you see where we are, for God's sake? We came at it another way. Don't you see?'

Lindholm said in a rather weak voice: 'I've never been up here before in my life.'

'Not you,' Stevenson shouted. 'Offdike.'

But Offdike was paying no attention. He was looking out over the immense valley which lay far below them. He pointed.

'What is it?' Lindholm demanded.

'There's the posse,' Offdike told them. 'And if I ain't mistaken, they're headed this way.'

Stevenson seemed to forget the old man. He hurried up the slope of the trail and joined Offdike. His gaze followed the pointing finger and now he seemed suddenly subdued as if he had been dropped into a pool of ice-cold water.

He swallowed. McAllister could see that he was sweating.

'How could they know?' he said.

Offdike said: 'It don't matter a goddam how they know. They're there, and before too long they'll be here.' He looked at McAllister and the girl and added: 'The damn fools. They're making sure you all die.'

McAllister said with a calm he did not feel: 'Stevenson, now's the time not to lose your head. You knock anybody off now, you'll hang for sure.'

In spite of the distant sight of the posse, however, Stevenson's rage was still turned on the old man. He walked to him, caught hold of his collar and hauled him to his feet. Then he dragged him, struggling, to Offdike.

'Offdike, when you open your eyes and look around you,' he said, 'you're going to want to kill this old bastard the same as me.'

Everybody there seemed to go still as Offdike looked around him. Before the truth hit the lank man, it hit McAllister. Or part of it. He was thinking . . . they must be near the Eagle's Nest. They were also near where Joe had hidden his gold, if the old man was telling the truth.

'Offdike's lean face was blank for a moment. Then slowly the heavy jaw dropped. He turned to look at Stevenson. Then at Joe Ramage.

'It can't be so,' he said. 'I can't believe it, Hank.'

He started to laugh.

Stevenson said: 'Cut it out, Offdike.' The tall man's laughter increased. He held one side and turned in the helplessness of his mirth. Then, as they listened, the note of his laughter changed. It began to sound with a note of hysteria.

Now Stevenson shouted: 'For Crissake, stop it.'

Offdike stopped. With hunched shoulders, he turned away and walked to a boulder. He sat down and stared at them with a curious listlessness.

'We wasted all these months,' he said. 'We got Carla there all the way from Chicago. Two of our men're dead. I killed the Kid myself. We thought we were rich.'

Lindholm said: 'I don't understand a thing about this. Shouldn't we move? I mean how long is it going to be before the posse reaches here?'

'Four, five hours,' McAllister said. 'The air's thin up here. They ain't as close as they look.'

Carla said: 'For God's sake tell us, Hank.' She was starting to look worried and a little scared.

Offdike's strange outburst seemed to have calmed Stevenson wonderfully.

'You're not going to believe this,' he said. 'And I can't blame you. I can hardly believe it myself. Maybe my imagination has over-reached itself.'

Joe Ramage said: 'You don't have to kill us now. You know the truth. I can't tell you anything you don't know already. There ain't no point in harming us now.'

Stevenson said: 'When we stopped the stage and took the gold off it, we were not robbing Joe Ramage here.'

Lindholm exclaimed: 'Who were you robbing then?'

Very quietly, Stevenson said: 'We were robbing ourselves.'

'What?'

McAllister reckoned he had never seen a man more surprised in his life. The banker looked shocked, horrified and stricken.

Carla said: 'Are you trying to tell us?'

Offdike said: 'There's an old saying "A wise man don't never shit on his own mudsill." We did our road jobs elsewhere. We lifted gold up in Montana. We stopped pack trains carrying the stuff in Idaho. We been shipping gold in here for years. The cash we took, we used for spending money. The gold we cached. We were ready to move on, so there wasn't any harm in us stopping the Black Horse stage. Our last job and we were clearing out. We'd heard about old Joe here and his gold. There ain't no ore in these hills. Only ours. Joe's been bringing out our gold. There was enough in Eagle's Nest to keep at least three of us as millionaires for the rest of our lives.'

McAllister was smiling hugely. 'Sweet, ain't it?' he said. He knew this was the moment.

Stevenson's control snapped again. He almost screamed: 'Shut your mouth, you stinking lawman, or I'll–'

McAllister said with cold intent, his eyes measuring and assessing: 'You've lost your nerve, Hank.' This was the only moment. Offdike was no longer behind him and could not see his hands, the bound hands which Allison had worked on all night and which had broken all her finger-nails. As he spoke his last word and Stevenson started towards him, he managed to get the last throng free. As the big man swung his carbine to smash the brass-bound butt into McAllister, the sheriff flicked the tough rawhide into his face like a whip lash. For that precious fraction of a second, Stevenson was caught in the small, sharp pain. McAllister hit him with all the power of his body. The edge of his hand caught Stevenson in the throat. Now the big man was between McAllister and Offdike.

Out of the corner of his eye, he saw Allison move. The girl was no more than a breath behind his own action. The couple of seconds it all took seemed like an eternity, for three lives hung on it.

The girl did exactly as he had told her.

First, she hurled herself at Joe's legs and knocked the light-weight old man from his feet. Second, she rolled out of the action and went clear off the trail. Then she had gone from sight and he heard her crashing noisily and no doubt painfully down the steep slope.

The only advantage they held over the man with the gun was the fact that they knew what they were going to do and he did not. They had also taken him by surprise. And now luck came into it. Offdike, on sitting down, had propped his Spencer carbine against the boulder beside him.

He was a mover. As soon as McAllister made his first move, he snatched at the weapon. By the time McAllister had felled Stevenson, the carbine was in his hands and he was jacking a round into the breech. He fired hastily, too hastily, as McAllister hurled himself down. By the time he had put another round into the breech, he saw McAllister disappearing over the edge.

Offdike was on his feet, running, shouting at Lindholm. The banker seemed as frozen to the spot as much as the girl Carla.

Offdike reached the edge of the trail and fired several shots into the scrub and brush below. Once, he turned with angry ferocity to Lindholm and bellowed: 'Can't you use a gun?'

Lindholm caught him by the arm. 'You'll bring the posse down on us with all this shooting.'

Offdike knocked him aside. He went on levering and

triggering furiously until the carbine was empty. Then he stood, staring blankly at the weapon. When at last he looked round, he saw that Stevenson was propped up on one elbow, vomiting. Lindholm stood with his revolver pointed at the prostrate and bewildered Joe Ramage.

Lindholm said with a desperate brightness: 'We still have one hostage.'

Offdike started looking around.

Carla asked: 'What're you looking for?'

Offdike said in a dead voice: 'Stevenson's carbine. McAllister took it.' This fact seemed to be more than he could bear. For a moment, utter hopelessness showed on his face. Finally, he pulled himself together and said: 'Lindholm, you and the girl catch up the horses. Move it now.' He walked over to Stevenson and said: 'Hank, get on your feet. This ain't no time to be sick. We have to cut our losses. I don't aim to cut down timber out of here without as much gold as the horses'll carry.'

Slowly, Stevenson hauled himself to his feet. His great bulk seemed shaken. He had shrunk a little. His complexion was grey and his eyes had a dead, stricken look about them. Very softly, as much to himself as Offdike, he said: 'I'll kill McAllister. Nobody ever laid a hand on me before.'

Offdike said: 'I daresay you'll get the chance.'

27

Those first few moments after they were free of their captors were painful and uncomfortable ones for McAllister and the girl. It was one of those times when they were willing to risk physical pain which ordinarily they would have shrunk from. Both knew that the chances were that they had leapt to their deaths; if the mountainside did not kill them, there were still the guns above.

Allison must have trusted McAllister's judgment, for she had thrown herself blindly from the trail, having no idea what awaited her. If she had known what she risked, maybe she would have stayed on the trail, where death was almost certain. As it was, she hit a slope so steep that it would have been impossible to stand on. Quite inexperienced in such activity, she was immediately completely out of control of herself. Rocks and brush tore at her, ripping clothes and flesh. Instinctively, as she bounced and was thrown onward, as she struck again and again, she tried to do two things at once. She wanted to protect her face and she wanted desperately to clutch at some firm object to halt her ever-increasing downward progress. Those moments were so full of violence and hurt that she did not feel any terror, just nature's protective instinct to save herself any way she could.

Once, her hands closed on the small gnarled trunk of a scrub oak which had somehow subsisted through the cold winters and on rocky terrain. She thought she was saved, but the downward pull was still too strong and her hands failed her. She rolled with dizzying speed and struck a small ledge, which seemed to toss her weightlessly into the gossamer top branches of a tiny stunted birch, which cushioned her, bent under her weight and then failed to stop her. She seemed to fall a long time. When she hit a grassy slope, her body seemed to disintegrate under the impact. She clutched at the coarse stems of the grass, found purchase and tried to rise; but here her body itself surrendered to the harsh treatment and collapsed.

She heard herself call: 'McAllister.' Whether she called loudly or softly, she did not know.

McAllister, when he went over the edge, knew, as much as any man could, what he was doing. But not even he could know what lay immediately below him. The evidence of his eyes was that he dived head-first into a sea of small tree-tops and brush.

He went through this with a crash that told him that they

were more substantial than they looked. No sooner was he through them than he hit rock, and it felt as if his whole body had been smashed in half by a giant blow. He began to roll violently, apparently out of control, and was aware that within seconds he might pitch out into space to be dashed to pieces on the rocks hundreds of feet below. Desperately, he turned the sideways roll into a shoulder roll and thus came out full length on the slope, head downwards. This brought his shoulder up hard with a small and twisted birch tree. His weight tore it almost from its roots, but the growth which had survived by clinging to almost bare rock through a dozen winters was not to be uprooted so easily. Only now did he realise that somebody was shooting downhill from above. He could hear the crash of a carbine, and the slugs tearing through the foliage. Once, a round hit a rock ten feet from him and whined away into the thin high air. Holding on to the tree, he allowed his body to slide downhill so that he could crane his head back to look in the direction of the trail. The brush and trees made it invisible to him.

He lay still, getting his breath and assessing the damage. The shooting stopped and he could hear the men's voices. He felt as if he had broken at least one rib. His clothes seemed to be ripped to shreds. In several places he could see blood where his flesh had been torn. He reckoned he would live – though in some discomfort.

First things first. He looked around for Stevenson's carbine and failed to see it. He swore, knowing that the weapon was essential to him. He heard the girl below, calling his name. At least she was alive. He started crawling back up the slope to search for the rifle. He did not enjoy that climb, because he ached considerably and every movement hurt, and because he expected any moment to be sighted from above and fired on.

Luck again came to his aid and he found the Spencer repeater, comparatively unharmed, a dozen feet above him. He rested and listened to the sounds from above. The horses were moving; a man shouted. He started down the hillside with enormous care. Once, he started a small cascade of rocks – and stayed still with held breath, waiting for the shot. But nothing came. Constantly twisting his head to look up, he went on down. Ten minutes later, he found the girl and was amazed to see her still alive. She had fallen a considerable distance. Her breathing was shallow and jerky, but there was no blood or froth on her lips. She was ashen, and her body lay twisted in an unnatural position.

He started to swear obscenely. The last thing he wanted was an injured girl to add to his difficulties. Very gingerly, he lifted her in his arms and started to walk with great difficulty down the slope. Taking several rests, he at last reached a narrow, steep ravine and clambered along it till he came to a rushing mountain torrent of crystal-clear ice-cold water. There was just enough flat ground to lay her down.

Thanks to the *barbiquejo*, he had not lost his hat. He filled it with water and bathed the girl's face. Then he trickled a little into her mouth. Shortly, she stirred and opened her eyes. For a moment, she stared blankly into his eyes, but when he smiled, she smiled back.

'Hey,' he said, 'you did pretty good back there.'

She said: 'Are we both still alive or is this heaven?'

'Heaven for me,' he said.

She said: 'This is no time for flirting, McAllister.'

'I never flirt, ma'am,' he said, and offered her his hand. 'I'm always dead serious about women. Anything else would be an insult. Let's see if we can get you on your feet. We should keep moving, and it's bad for my presence of mind to keep carrying you.'

She was hurt and she winced when she tried to get up, but his voice had reassured her. When she was on her feet, she leaned against him and he put an arm around her. He could have wished Joe and his gold and the villains a hundred miles off. When he kissed her gently on the temple, her sigh changed its note. She leaned back in his arms and looked up at him.

'You'd best get me out of this safe and sound, McAllister,' she said softly. 'That kiss was kind of nice, and I'd like some more of the same without the chance of gunmen descending on us.'

Holding her hand, he started to find them a difficult trail

down the ravine. He reckoned they were working their way east again. She walked stiffly and in pain at first, but she was a hardy girl and she soon settled down to walking. As they travelled, he watched the skyline, and every now and then stopped to listen. He told her: 'We could be in a pretty bad fix. We didn't eat for a good while and we don't have any food. Maybe that's the posse we saw and maybe it wasn't. And I'm dead set on getting old Joe from them alive.'

'I'll go along with that.'

'I'll have to hide you somewhere safe, then get to work.'

She stopped in her tracks. 'Where you go, I go. I'm too scared to do anything else. I don't know these mountains and if you're hurt or – if you're hurt, maybe nobody'll know where I am.'

He said: 'I never saw a girl less scared in my life.'

28

McAllister's escape with the girl seemed to have transformed Offdike's character. Now he was all worry and fret. His alarm touched Stevenson, and he too lost his calm. Both men were irritable and edgy. Maybe they had their minds on nothing but saving the gold, any of the gold which they had hidden up here over the years. Lindholm was in a maze, repeating to himself: 'I just can't make out how such a thing could happen.'

They were in the saddle now, riding as fast as the rough trail would allow. Once, Stevenson stopped to put his glass on the posse below, but found they were no longer in view.

'Maybe it wasn't the posse we saw. Maybe it wasn't them at all,' he said.

'It don't matter one way or the other,' Offdike told him.

'We have to move fast. Remember, that bastard McAllister is out there some place with a loaded carbine. Your loaded carbine.'

'One man,' Stevenson said shortly, 'with eight rounds of ammunition. A fat lot of good that'll do him.' But he did not mean it and none of them believed he did. The thought of McAllister spooked him more than the posse.

They sighted the cave near noon and now Offdike stopped again to produce his glass. This time he found the posse. He couldn't make out any great deal. There were six men there, he said, and they were coming on fast. They were well-mounted and had come much further than he thought possible.

'Jesus, we got to move, Hank.'

Now it seemed that their hurry became something of a desperate scramble. Lindholm and Carla saw the cave for the first time, a massive hole rent in the peak. This itself was Eagle's Nest. The road agents' cache was off to one side of it. When they reached it, Lindholm saw that over the years, the various outlaws who had forted up here had built a stout wall of rocks. Within the confines of this wall, they drew rein and Stevenson said: 'Offdike, you stay here and keep a look out for McAllister. You others bring the horses and we'll start packing.'

Offdike said: 'All right. Joe stays here. McAllister only has to show himself around here and the old crowbait is dead.' Stevenson led the way into the cave with Lindholm saying at his elbow: 'We shall have to come to some agreement how we're going to divide the gold.'

Too easily for Lindholm's liking, Stevenson said: 'Sure. You and Carla don't have a thing to worry about, Howie.' The banker knew that he and Carla were in acute danger. But the nearness of the gold held him. He had come too far, burned too many boats and taken too many risks to leave without enough to last him the rest of his life, or at least set him up in a good business in some place that did not know him. He and Carla would have a good life together. The girl was genuinely fond of him.

They turned into the side cave and Stevenson found a

lamp and lit it. They went forward no more than another thirty feet or so and came into what seemed to be a vast chamber. At once they could see that men had used the place for a number of years. There were bunks, boxes, parfleches and piled sacks.

Stevenson was all business now, telling Lindholm and Carla just what had to be done. Lindholm, who had a deep moral objection to physical exertion, already saddle-sore and bone weary, was sweating and miserable as he laboured in the shadowy gloom of the cave, but he put his back into it because he wanted that gold. Warning bells were sounding in his head. He felt that both Stevenson and Offdike, now they knew that Joe Ramage had been stealing their gold, would see that neither he nor Carla had their share. He was no hero, but he meant to come out of this with gold and the girl. He had dreamed for too long to accept defeat easily.

Once, when Stevenson led a laden horse outside the cave, Lindholm turned to the girl. Her face was sweaty and dust-caked, but she still looked beautiful to him. He laid a hand on her arm.

'Have you changed your mind, Carla?' he asked.

'About what?' She sounded surprised.

'About us sticking together.'

She smiled. 'I seemed to remember something a little stronger than that. Like marriage.'

'Of course. But have you changed your mind?'

She kissed him. 'No. I haven't!'

'All right, now. Be ready. Offdike and Stevenson do not mean to play fair with us.'

'I'm damn sure they don't.'

They talked together until Offdike came back to take Stevenson's place. The three of them sweated in the cave for another hour and all the horses were carrying all they could. Now, Lindholm said with more calm than he felt: 'Carla and I are not blind or dumb, Hank. You have packed gold on all the horses except three. It looks as if you intend to leave one of us behind. Which one?'

Stevenson turned.

His right hand held his belt-gun. He said: 'We're leaving

two behind, Howie. You and the girl. We're taking old Joe along with us as insurance. You can have all the gold that's left here – if you can tote it out.'

Carla said: 'We expected something like this, Hank.'

'Then it comes as no surprise. We kept our word. You have your share.'

Carla said: 'You've both turned out to be the cheap bastards we thought you.'

Offdike ignored her. 'I'll take your weapons, just in case.' He rammed the muzzle of his gun into Lindholm's belly and lifted the banker's gun from leather.

'You realise, Hank, you could be leaving us for the law. We're afoot. Neither of us could survive in the wild.'

Stevenson said: 'Too bad. At least we didn't kill you. Thank the Lord for small mercies.' He stuck Lindholm's gun behind his belt and walked out, leading the last horse. Lindholm started towards the exit, but the girl laid a hand on his arm to restrain him.

'Let them go,' she said. 'The law will follow the horses. Let's take what gold we can carry and quietly lose ourselves in the landscape.'

He kissed her and said: 'Carla, you're a wonderful woman and the best thing that ever happened to me.'

29

As soon as Offdike stepped out into the clear sunlight, the shot came. The flat slam of the rifle echoed and re-echoed through the hills, so that neither Offdike nor Stevenson knew where it came from. It hit the face of the rock at least six feet from Offdike and sang away into the blue.

Stevenson, who had been crouched down beside Joe

Ramage behind the rocky wall, was on his feet in an instant, shouting: 'Let's get the hell out of here.' Offdike did not need any second bidding, but at once started to fix the pack-animals in a string, while Stevenson drove the old man in front of him, telling him to get into the saddle fast or he'd put a bullet through his head. Another shot came, but it was no nearer to a human target than the first. But close enough to hasten their efforts.

'Which way now?' Offdike demanded as he vaulted into the saddle.

'West,' Stevenson shouted, swinging astride. They both laid on quirts and got their precious train moving. They headed for the downward trail, moving at a reckless speed for so difficult a descent, Offdike towing the lead horse, Stevenson urging the string of animals from the rear. They came down through the rocks and hit the first timberline. Offdike could see the posse toiling slowly to the south of them, still a couple of hours off. He pointed to them and shouted back to Stevenson. He turned in the saddle to see Stevenson blowing the posse a kiss and laughing.

It was at this point, when Offdike turned his face to the west, that Stevenson started in the saddle in sudden alarm and surprise. There was a man running beside his horse. He saw that it was McAllister; but that was impossible, because McAllister had fired two shots at the cave, which meant that he must have been to the south . . . As the truth came to Stevenson, as he realised that it was the girl who had fired the shots, as he reached hastily for the gun at his side, something struck very hard across his chest. McAllister's crude club, nothing more than a twisted bough of scrub-oak, took him out of the saddle. He was a badly hurt man before he hit ground. His horse started to pitch, and away it went, following the others. Stevenson made one more effort to draw his gun, but this time the club caught him on the crown of his head.

As his partner disappeared round the bend in the trail, Stevenson's wrists were lashed together with all the speed of a calf being hogtied by a skilled man. When he came to his senses, he was alone in the world and McAllister had gone from sight. He enjoyed but one thought: *I should never have messed with amateurs.*

He did not know it then, but he was more fortunate than his partner. Offdike reached a mountain torrent and found his progress slowed by the difficulty of the crossing. Turning to shout back to Stevenson, he failed to find him. To Joe Ramage, who was riding with his horse tied in the middle of the string, he said: 'Where the hell did Hank get to?' and Joe replied: 'How in hell should I know?' Which was a good question, because he had neither heard nor seen Stevenson's meeting of his comeuppance.

Offdike might be puzzled and alarmed, but he did not lose sight of his priorities, which were to get out of this alive and in the company of his gold. He therefore raked his horse with spurs and urged it across the water. He was in mid-stream and having the greatest difficulty in keeping his horse on its feet, when he looked up and saw a man standing on the far side of the stream with a gun pointed at him. His reaction was much the same as his partner's – that the sheriff could not possibly be here. He also slapped his right hand down on the butt of his gun. It was a suicide move, of course, but Offdike three years before had successfully drawn against a naked gun down in El Paso, Texas. Offdike was fast and he was accurate. To give him due credit, he not only drew his gun, but he also got off a shot. His aim was spoiled, however, by the fact that McAllister's gun had also gone off and a bullet was lodged in his chest. He grabbed leather with his left hand and fought to raise his gun for a second shot, but McAllister's second bullet hit him within an inch of the first and lifted him out of the saddle, for his grip on the saddle-horn was by then quite feeble. He hit the surface of the stream with a great splash. His horse tried to pitch, but lost its footing and went down. The strength of the torrent rolled the animal over, but it fought to regain its footing and managed to do so. McAllister waded into the water, leaning against its strength, and led the horse back across to Joe Ramage.

The old man looked down at McAllister and said: 'Jesus, it took you long enough. I don't know what the hell lawmen're coming to these days. Do I have to sit here all day before you cut me loose?'

McAllister said: 'You can stay up there all day for all I care. Unless you can defend yourself against the charge of being a goddam old swindling son-of-a-bitch.'

'I don't know what you're talking about,' Joe said.

'You know what I'm talking about,' said McAllister. 'About you stealing the road agents' gold and getting half Black Horse working itself into a sweat on behalf of the poor old millionaire.'

Joe smiled like an evil old angel. 'Aw, that,' he said. 'That ain't so, Rem.'

'Prove it,' said McAllister.

'Nothing easier,' said Joe. 'Follow this here stream down about a half-mile and you'll find where I've panned and dug for three, four years. I don't care who knows now. I got all the gold I need.' He cackled with delight. 'You mean I had you fooled too?'

McAllister snarled: 'You stay tied till you quit grinning. You goddam millionaires're all the same.'

30

Mark Tully said: 'McAllister, I reckon this time you used up the last of your luck.' The posse sat around toasting deer-meat on sticks over the fire. Well, half the posse sat around; the other half had spurred for home to fetch picks, shovels, pans, anything to hand which would help them lift some of the gold before the whole country heard of it and there was a stampede. McAllister rose abruptly and walked into the moonlight to the edge of the creek. A moment later, Mark Tully was at his elbow.

'Hell, Rem,' he said, 'was it something I said?'

McAllister looked surprised. 'No. Just I killed a man. It don't get any easier, Mark.'

Tully nodded. 'Me too. I've had my bellyful. That's why I ain't too eager for posses and such.'

'I've had my fill of killing other folk's snakes. Time they got around to killing their own. From here on in, I stick with horses.'

'Still, times like that have their compensations.'

McAllister grinned. 'You mean half the gold dug up here will be spent at your place?'

'No, I was thinking of old Joe's girl.'

'What were you thinking?'

'She ain't took her eyes off you since you got into camp. How's it I never get around to hiding out in the brush with a lovely girl?'

McAllister turned and looked back at the camp fire. He saw that Allison was gone. One of the young possemen was missing too. Hell, he thought, that was the way it went. The young were attracted to the young.

'I'm too damned old,' McAllister said. 'Got to face it.'

Mark walked chuckling back to the fire, saying: 'That'll be the day.'

McAllister strolled along the creek bank. He had not taken three paces when he walked into somebody.

She said: 'What's this about being too old?'

'Me,' he said. 'I'm too old.'

She reached up a cool hand and laid it against his face. She said: 'You weren't too old when you were comforting me out in the brush.'

'You were kind of upset,' he said. 'I couldn't think of anything else.'

She laughed and put her arms around his neck. 'I'm upset now,' she said. He put his arms around her waist and pulled her gently against him. With her mouth almost against his, she whispered: 'You're a great comfort to a girl.'

'Ain't I,' he said, and their mouths and their bodies came together.

THE END

FICTION

GENERAL

☐ Chains	Justin Adams	£1.25
☐ Secrets	F. Lee Bailey	£1.25
☐ The Last Liberator	John Clive	£1.25
☐ Wyndward Passion	Norman Daniels	£1.35
☐ Rich Little Poor Girl	Terence Feely	£1.50
☐ Abingdon's	Michael French	£1.25
☐ The Moviola Man	Bill and Colleen Mahan	£1.25
☐ Running Scared	Gregory Mcdonald	85p
☐ Gossip	Marc Olden	£1.25
☐ The Red Raven	Lilli Palmer	£1.25
☐ The Sounds of Silence	Judith Richards	£1.00
☐ Summer Lightning	Judith Richards	£1.25
☐ The Hamptons	Charles Rigdon	£1.35
☐ The Affair of Nina B.	Simmel	95p
☐ The Berlin Connection	Simmel	£1.50
☐ The Cain Conspiracy	Simmel	£1.20
☐ Double Agent—Triple Cross	Simmel	£1.35
☐ Celestial Navigation	Anne Tyler	£1.00
☐ Searching for Caleb	Anne Tyler	£1.00

WESTERN BLADE SERIES

☐ No. 1 The Indian Incident	Matt Chisholm	75p
☐ No. 2 The Tucson Conspiracy	Matt Chisholm	75p
☐ No. 3 The Laredo Assignment	Matt Chisholm	75p
☐ No. 4 The Pecos Manhunt	Matt Chisholm	75p
☐ No. 5 The Colorado Virgins	Matt Chisholm	85p
☐ No. 6 The Mexican Proposition	Matt Chisholm	85p
☐ No. 7 The Arizona Climax	Matt Chisholm	85p
☐ No. 8 The Nevada Mustang	Matt Chisholm	85p
☐ No. 9 The Montana Deadlock	Matt Chisholm	85p
☐ No. 10 The Cheyenne Trap	Matt Chisholm	95p
☐ No. 11 The Navaho Trail	Matt Chisholm	95p

WAR

☐ The Andersen Assault	Peter Leslie	£1.25
☐ Killers Under a Cruel Sky	Peter Leslie	£1.25
☐ Jenny's War	Jack Stoneley	£1.25

NAVAL HISTORICAL

☐ HMS Bounty	John Maxwell	£1.00
☐ The Mary Celeste	John Maxwell	£1.00
☐ The Baltic Convoy	Showell Styles	95p

SCIENCE FICTION

☐ Clash by Night	Henry Kuttner	95p
☐ Drinking Sapphire Wine	Tanith Lee	£1.25
☐ Journey	Marta Randall	£1.00

NON-FICTION

GENERAL

☐ **The Chinese Mafia**	Fenton Bresler	£1.50
☐ **Here Comes Everybody**	Anthony Burgess	£1.75
☐ **Basil Ede's Birds**	Dougall & Ede	£4.95
☐ **Strange Deaths**	John Dunning	£1.50
☐ **Truly Murderous**	John Dunning	£1.50
☐ **Ielfstan's Place**	Richard Girling	£1.95

TRAVEL

☐ **The Complete Traveller**	Joan Bakewell	£1.95
☐ **Camping in Comfort**	Dymphna Byrne	£1.75
☐ **A Walk Around the Lakes**	Hunter Davies	£1.95
☐ **Weekend Cycling**	Christa Gausden	£1.95
☐ **Britain by Train**	Patrick Goldring	£1.75
☐ **England by Bus**	Elizabeth Gundrey	£1.75
☐ **Staying Off the Beaten Track** *(revised edition)*	Elizabeth Gundrey	£2.95
☐ **Weekend Walking**	Roger Smith	£1.95
☐ **Britain at Your Feet**	Wickers & Pedersen	£1.75

BIOGRAPHY/AUTOBIOGRAPHY

☐ **All You Needed Was Love**	John Blake	£1.50
☐ **The Queen Mother Herself**	Helen Cathcart	£1.25
☐ **Clues to the Unknown**	Robert Cracknell	£1.50
☐ **George Stephenson**	Hunter Davies	£1.50
☐ **William Wordsworth**	Hunter Davies	£2.50
☐ **The Family Story**	Lord Denning	£1.95
☐ **Nelson**	Harry Edgington	£1.50
☐ **The Admiral's Daughter**	Victoria Fyodorova	£1.75
☐ **Nancy Astor**	John Grigg	£2.95
☐ **Monty**	Nigel Hamilton	£4.95
☐ **Fifty Years with Mountbatten**	Charles Smith	£1.25
☐ **Maria Callas**	Arianna Stassinopoulos	£1.75
☐ **Swanson on Swanson**	Gloria Swanson	£2.95

NAME ....

ADDRESS ....

....

Write to Hamlyn Paperbacks Cash Sales, PO Box 11, Falmouth, Cornwall TR10 9EN.

Please indicate order and enclose remittance to the value of the cover price plus:

U.K.: Please allow 45p for the first book plus 20p for the second book and 14p for each additional book ordered, to a maximum charge of £1.63.

B.F.P.O. & EIRE: Please allow 45p for the first book plus 20p for the second book and 14p per copy for the next 7 books, thereafter 8p per book.

OVERSEAS: Please allow 75p for the first book and 21p per copy for each additional book.

Whilst every effort is made to keep prices low it is sometimes necessary to increase cover prices and also postage and packing rates at short notice. Hamlyn Paperbacks reserve the right to show new retail prices on covers which may differ from those previously advertised in the text or elsewhere.